Anna Shipton

Hidden Springs

Anna Shipton

Hidden Springs

ISBN/EAN: 9783337368968

Printed in Europe, USA, Canada, Australia, Japan

Cover: Foto ©Andreas Hilbeck / pixelio.de

More available books at **www.hansebooks.com**

BY

ANNA SHIPTON,

AUTHOR OF

"TELL JESUS," "THE PROMISE AND THE PROMISER,"
"THE LOST BLESSING," ETC., ETC., ETC.

WILLARD TRACT REPOSITORY,

BEACON HILL PLACE, BOSTON.
239 FOURTH AVENUE, NEW YORK.
921 ARCH STREET, PHILADELPHIA.
31 PATERNOSTER SQUARE, LONDON.

PREFACE.

THE simple incidents in the following pages have been extracted from my journals. I have chosen those that concern the habitual occurrences of life; for every day's need requires the Bread that cometh down from heaven.

If we seek the understanding of the Lord and his will only in what we esteem important events, or particular seasons of extremity, we shall miss that fellowship which He is willing to give us at all times. Moreover, by a frequent contemplation of his dealings we are drawn to his Word, the lamp and light to our feet: "God is not mocked: for whatsoever a man soweth, that shall he also reap." If we gather up the remembrance of his hourly care, his readiness to succor in trial and temptation, his willingness to cleanse and forgive, we shall gain a knowledge of *Himself*, and learn "the things that are freely given us of God"; and the faith and patience by which we inherit the promises will make them our own.

The experience of the inner life can only be received by those who have an inner life. "The natural man receiveth not the things of the Spirit of God: for they are foolishness unto him: neither can he know them, because they are spiritually discerned." (1 Cor. ii. 14.) Therefore, for much of the secret experience of that life we must be content to be misunderstood and despised. But in our desert journey, there are those among the hidden ones of God whose harps are tuned to give responsive echoes to such experience; for much that is impossible to convey in words can be received only by sympathy.

The weakness of Christian life to-day, its rapidity and its commotion, has still in its hidden depths a vain yearning for something more to fill it; and setting a line of demarcation on what is religious and what is not religious, men make to themselves two paths, and therefore as it were two lives: the one the old nature's life, and the other a religious life without unction and without enjoyment. Thirsty and weary, they are blind to the fountain that flows beside them; to the rivers among the rocks, the pools in the wilderness, and wells in the desert.

From the other side of the Atlantic, my broken utterances have called forth echoes from strangers' harps, that have made music to my heart in many a day of rejection, many an enforced silent hour, many a rough journey; and these pages contain answers to various letters from pilgrim brothers, whose faces I shall never look on until this mortal body shall put on incorruption. I ask them, and all of my readers who by the grace of God may find water in the channels I have striven to delve with my weak hands, to pray for a blessing: if the Enemy has stopped one up, or filled it with clay, that in the strength of the Lord of Hosts He may cast it forth; that there may be no impediment to the flow of the Living Water that the Lord has promised as the portion of those that believe in Him. (John vii. 38.)

The copyright of this my American edition I have conceded to Dr. Charles Cullis, of Boston; and the prayers of many, in England and elsewhere, follow its circulation in prayer and blessing.

> Make me, Lord, as a river,
>   A river of health and joy;
> A river to flow forever,
>   When cisterns of earth are dry.
> Bearing a brother's burden
>   Over the dark sea's flood;
> Filling a thousand channels,
>   To gladden the City of God.

CONTENTS.

HIDDEN SPRINGS;

OR,

LIFE HID WITH CHRIST IN GOD.

CHAPTER I.

RECOLLECTING HOUR.

"Thou shalt *remember* all the way which the Lord thy God led thee these forty years in the wilderness, to humble thee, and to prove thee, to know what was in thine heart." — Deut. viii. 2.

"Only fear the Lord, and serve Him in truth: for *consider* how great things He hath done for you." — 1 Sam. xii. 24.

"Take heed to thyself, and keep thy soul diligently, *lest thou forget* the things which thine eyes have seen, and lest they depart from thy heart all the days of thy life." — Deut. iv. 9.

"CONSIDER"; so spake God by his prophet Haggai, so speaks He to-day by his Word. It was his own people, not aliens, that He reproved. They were content to dwell at ease and leave the service of the Lord, as seen in the building of his house, which is the service of the sanctuary. They were seeking their own pleasure, which brought them no profit, while his service was neglected. "Consider your ways," according to the command of the Lord ; for " because of mine house that is waste, and ye run every man unto his own house. Therefore the heaven over you is stayed from dew, and the earth is stayed from her fruit." (Hag. i. 9, 10.) Why is there no blessing on the service in which they have engaged, no result that endures, no fruit that remaineth?

The Lord sends his message from " the Lord of *hosts*," thus reminding his lukewarm followers of his power to help them. The same message stands good for to-day. Nothing proclaims more vividly how easy to be entreated is our gracious Lord, than these reproofs of his often rebellious and backsliding people. Immediately the remnant fear before Him, and hasten to obey Him ; He comforts and strengthens them with the Word which sends life into every prostrate soul, " I am with you." What more do we need for service or for suffering? What more do we need than to realize that our enemies are his enemies? The Lord of hosts is with us! He also has made known to us his future kingdom, his power, and his glory, with his crowning blessing of peace, and a promise of the beauty and the glory of that house which He has called *us* to build, — a glory far greater than that of the former house. He does not send an angel-legion to do the work for his people, yet that He could well have done ; it was the work *in* them He needed. Therefore He acts on the spirit of Zerubbabel, and Joshua the son of Josedech, giving at the same time to the remnant the desire to labor in earnest for that which should bring forth glory to God.

He bade them "Be strong." and they were strong. "Work, for I am with you," said the Lord of hosts, and they worked. He reminds them of his covenant when they came out of Egypt; of his faithfulness, his presence among them: and bids them " fear not "

" Consider " runs through all the Lord's dealings with his remnant; and equally through his dealings with *us* to-day. He bids them look back on their poverty, while they labored in very vanity for *themselves*, and spent their money for *themselves*, and spent their money for that which was not bread. He tells them the purpose of his chastening, — purposes of love to bring them nearer to Himself, that they may trust Him, and apprehend Him intelligently. And now that they have *considered* and turned from idols to serve the living and true God, their fig-trees and their pomegranates, their vines and their olives, which have not brought forth, receive his blessing. which can alone bring prosperity, so that their earthly fruitfulness should increase when their labor was bestowed upon that which pleased the Lord. While they obey his voice and work in his service, He commands the blessing on that which they leave for his sake ; so that not only they lacked nothing, but they were richer in trusting the Lord than in laboring for themselves! Is it not thus to-day, with those who have left all to follow Jesus?

He promises that their enemies which are his enemies should be overthrown ; and that He would destroy the strength of the kingdom of the heathen, their chariots also, and those that ride in them ! And in that day of

crowning grace He declares, " *My* servant shall be as
a signet"; and this. not because of his labor, — not
because of his strength, which was the gift of the Lord,
from his presence with him: no! but because grace
does all. " Because I have *chosen* thee."

Forgotten mercies are lost blessings, therefore the
Lord calls us to " consider." If we were not so busy
outwardly, we should oftener raise our Ebenezer to the
glory of God, and the refreshment and encouragement
of our fellow-travellers. When the Lord reminded
Jacob of the past, when he fled a fugitive from his en-
raged brother, He was still leading him about and
instructing him, as He does his wilderness family to-
day. He will not have his children, whom He is about
to bless yet more richly, either uninstructed or forget-
ful of the mercies already bestowed on them. " Whoso
is wise and will observe these things, even they shall
understand the loving-kindness of the Lord."

Do we not arise girded for travel or trial or service,
when we have tarried again at Bethel, which has
become a Peniel to our lonely and distracted heart?
Shall I not draw nearer to *Him* who answered me in
the day of my distress, and was with me in the way
that I went, or when I recalled his promise given, and
the first wondrous revelation of his love, even until
to-day?

The Lord bade Jacob go to Bethel, and Jacob went;
and " the Lord appeared to him," conferred on him his
new name, and enlarged his promises. Thus it will
ever be in the walk of faith, if we apprehend Him.
But for this we must " consider." Until graciously

reminded of it, Jacob seemed to have forgotten that he had vowed a vow unto the Lord, that if He would give him the bare necessaries of life, and bring him back in peace, then the Lord should be his God. God gave him abundance. He had protected and delivered him. He confirmed the promises of his forefathers to him and gave him individual blessings for himself; yet Jacob forgot the sacrifice of a thankful heart, and only at the close of his long and eventful life did he bear testimony of the wondrous love and faithfulness of Jehovah, the Angel that had redeemed him from all evil.

The first sacrifice of Jacob that we read of is when he is separated from the people with whom he dwelt, like Abraham when Lot had gone forth to the plain of Sodom.

It is a separate people that sing the song of Moses and the Lamb, when death is behind them, and they can follow the Lamb whithersoever He goeth, and rejoice that they are counted worthy to suffer for his sake.

Those who have dealings with the Lord can best proclaim his love and power, and declare, "Verily God hath heard me; He hath attended to the voice of my prayer" (Ps. lxvi.); and another will hear the song of praise, and exclaim, "Then why not to *mine?*"

Who that has realized the faithfulness of the Lord does not set up his Ebenezer on the trackless way he has journeyed in life, hid in Christ with God?

Why are so many silent in his praise? "Oh that men would praise the Lord for his goodness, and for his wonderful works to the children of men!" (Ps. cvii. 21.) "Let them sacrifice the sacrifices of thanksgiving, and declare his works with rejoicing." Christ is our sacrifice; Christ is our praise!

If we are content to share our sorrows and our trials with our brethren only, they may be used as ministers of consolation and instruction; but who that has been shut up alone to the sympathy of the Man of Sorrows (like as to the communion in the joys in which none other shares) does not know that the golden ladder of promise, revealed to him in the darkest desert restingplace, was to him the very gate of heaven, a landmark for eternity, that remaineth forever?

Why are Christians so afraid of solitude? Why do they shun the still hour which is so often offered and rejected? If they travel, they must take their book or newspaper; or if waiting, must seek some object of interest to fill the passing hour: but how seldom is the long journey or the forced seclusion taken as the opportunity of spreading their souls before the Lord, as a season of separation or communion which might prepare them for any testimony or service to which He may have called them! Some can go so far as to seek for pastime: as if time did not pass fast enough without such aids; as if we were not gliding down the stream of time into eternity, and every moment a golden grain, lost or gained.

Curiosity is one of the worms that destroy spiritual buds and blossoms, so that they bring forth no fruit. The mind becomes scattered, weak, and idle in the search of the imperishable riches; habits of idle conver-

sation are formed ; and questions that scarcely require
an answer, or subjects fruitless of any solid good. are
entertained, — when each believer might have contrib-
uted something to the divine record (Mal. iii. 16).
" Pleasant pictures " are thus gathered in the inner
galleries of imagination, and the mind, filled with useless
materials, is wearied with a burden which is of no value.

When we reflect on the brief time allotted to each
of us for our education here, to fit us for the position
which the King of glory has ordained us to fill, it
quickens our desire to attain to that which He sets
before us, individually. For this we must believe in
the love of God, and consider his ways, and believe
that all the circumstances of our daily life have this
end in view ; a lesson not learned in a day, and when
learned, often overgrown with suspicious and fears of
righteous judgment for our own transgressions, rather
than the gratitude for the way of escape and the
cleansing fountain, when so much remains for our consideration and praise.

To dwell on this long-suffering and tenderness of
our Father, this gift of Jesus, our life given and sustained, and blessings past numbering, is a source of
thanksgiving forever upspringing, if we accustom ourselves to find our pleasure with Him. There can be no
fruit, save in abiding in Him who is the root of all
fruitfulness ; but thus learning to apprehend Him, we
can better trust in his love and care. It is a sorrowful
retrospection to all of us, that we have trusted in Him
so little, and confided in Him so fitfully.

Is it because our mind is more occupied with worldly

interests, or our own sins and sorrows, that we are so often disinclined to *rest* in his presence, and that we so seldom sit before Him, like David, and review all his promises for our future, all his wondrous works in our behalf? Surely the most sorrowful reminiscences of our past should have a holy influence on our lives, if they have been used by the Lord to bring us into the path in which He had ordained us to walk, — nay, that perhaps in the first place were used to bring us to his feet.

David sat before the Lord. Why do we so seldom rest with Him in happy contemplation of his nearness? The communion of saints is no fable. We sit in assured fellowship with our dearest friend, thankful for an uninterrupted hour of intimate communion, jealous of interruption, feeling when we separate how much we have left unsaid, and longing for the time to renew it, — overcoming obstacles that would bar us from it, or patiently enduring, so that in the end the object of our desires may be granted us. I feel assured, that if our hearts were *set on Him* who is more willing to be all to us, this would be much more frequently our position with our unalterable Friend; for our knowledge of Him must spring out of watching unto prayer and fellowship with Him.

In a time of much pressure of occupation I prayed the Lord for an *hour of recollection*, when I might rest in his presence. I was hungry and thirsty and weary in my wilderness march; a long summer's day had gone down, and yet not half an hour had been mine when I could calmly sit before Him and " consider."

The last effort of my weariness was to keep an appointment with a lady who resided in a neighboring square. The sun was going down when I reached her door, and heard with dismay that she was not within. The servant, on reading my card, at once begged me to enter, as her mistress entreated me to await her speedy return.

Certain of my own punctuality, and vexed at my detention, I followed the servant up-stairs, inwardly chafed at the last hour of the day being thus wasted. I remember that I sat down almost sullenly in the drawing-room, the windows of which faced the west.

As I sat, my eyes rested on the gorgeous sunset before me, mirrored in the broad ocean that now lay like a crimson lake, with the wavelets of the rising tide crested with gold, while the dark-purple clouds seemed like the curtains of the inner sanctuary which they veiled. All was still, as if nature reposed in praise.

As I gazed on the scene so unexpectedly opened before me, my spirit became peaceful, my body rested, and my love to the Great Creator and mine, penetrated my inmost being.

A season of unlooked-for communion followed. The lady was detained *exactly an hour* longer than she anticipated; and I recognized the tender mercy and loving-kindness of my faithful Lord, in not withholding his blessing because of my impatient spirit, but having pity upon my yearning heart and weary frame. He gave me his presence, in full of all my desires.

Often when my eyes rest on such a sunset, with its delicate lines of opal and its amethyst curtains, in the

glory of the eventide, my heart melts at the remem
brance of his goodness, and my "recollecting hour"
comes back, fresh as though it were yesterday, and
whispers to my soul, " I am the Lord, I change not."
Yes! if we desired such seasons, and our hearts were
set on *Him*, such would be granted us ; and though I
believe the power and presence of the Lord are often
more *sensibly* maintained when consciously serving Him
than in days spent in abstract meditation on the Word,
yet *some* silent hours are indispensable for the further-
ance of his service, by which needful rest and an appre-
hension of heaven are maintained, — as one occupied
within his office or at his desk, or even in manual
labor, would seek a moment's refreshment in cessation
from work, or with a body jaded by fatigue, would
enter the door of his home for the smile that waited
him, to gather strength for the battle of life. The
physician, the man of letters, the merchant, those
engaged in the instruction of others, the busy shop-
keeper, the artisan, the dressmaker, the lawyer, all
may find that little season in the day to sit before
the Lord.

Even if the body be exhausted, the mind jaded, the
spirit depressed and galled beneath the cross of the
day, yet we are not there to give to God anything but
what He is willing to take, — our weakness and our
weariness and our needs, — and we are there to receive.
He whom we desire is there to glorify Himself, by
restoring our souls, washing our travel-soiled feet,
anointing us anew, and bracing us again for the journey. Praise may fail, prayer may seem to be no

prayer; but in our inmost being we desire *Him*, and the Lord is at hand! " Tell me, O Thou whom my soul loveth, where thou feedest, where thou makest thy flock to rest at noon." He is found of them that seek Him *not*, — will He hide Himself from his dear, weary, tempted ones, who serve Him and long after Him? He gives not according to *our* merits, but according to the merits of his sinless Son; not regarding our peevish murmurs, but our longing to approach Him though feeling acutely our own unfitness. He will not fail thee!

The Father knoweth that we have need of such things; He remembereth that we are dust! I set this before a man of business, who, above his daily labor, was ever actively engaged in helping others, so that he had not so much as time to eat bread. He was jaded and distressed from lack of communion. He replied to my argument, " It is almost impossible, in the press of business, to find an hour, or half an hour, to seek the Lord thus quietly and alone."

' But if you asked the Lord to *give* you even a quarter of an hour," I suggested. He smiled and inquired, " Will *you* ask Him to give it to me to-day?" I promised to do so; and when at noon I sought repose for myself, I prayed the same glorious Lord to remember my overworked, weary brother. We met in the evening, and I inquired, " And did you find a season of rest with the Lord to-day?"

" Yes, indeed!" he replied, with animation. " A gentleman called to see me on a matter of business at mid-day, and when it was arranged, I was locking my office to leave, when I heard a quick step along the passage. My visitor had returned, saying as he approached me. 'Could we not pray together?' We did pray, and the presence of the Lord strengthened me for all that awaited me the succeeding part of the day." It was the same hour in which I had asked for refreshment for my thirsty friend. "I will feed my flock, and I will cause them to lie down, saith the Lord God." We must remember the prayers we have breathed and the vows we have vowed when the Lord's hand was on us, and the promises we have made when we have aforetime considered our ways ; for from lack of this we often miss the knowledge of the purpose of a new phase of trial sent to prove us. Again and again we find affliction a " strange thing " (1 Pet. iv. 12). Yet in the end some fruit will be seen for ourselves or others, for which we thank God, and take courage.

I am not referring to those deep mysteries in every life hid with God, for the solution of which we must wait, and leave it confidingly in his hands to unravel through the ages of eternity, but of those we have already recognized as lessons from which He has taught us to profit: for the rest, He has promised, " What thou knowest not now thou shalt know hereafter." *Now* the heart may quiver and bleed in reviewing the past ; yet if we can recognize his hand in it, or his supporting grace through it, we shall find an answer to our prayer for a deeper *knowledge of Himself.* Let us not be afraid to look back on the pit and the prison, used by the Lord of hosts to bring us to the place appointed in his kingdom. Even if our sorrows have been caused by our own inherent sinfulness. and wrought out by our own wilfulness, there will always be seen some token of his love and his care; something in which mercy has been evident, some greater wrong from which He has defended us, some temptation whose disastrous power had nigh overwhelmed us, all swept away at his word; some dark providence in which his hand has at last been shown evidently for our protection, — all these remembered mercies will ultimately give us cause to praise.

How often has He placed us in some uncongenial society to hedge up our way to Himself! How often an indisposition (not a dropsy or a fever) has set us apart and *alone*, that we may more entirely learn his will, seek his face, and sit before Him; and sometimes that we may consider his love, and be melted by his mercies. or remember from whence we have fallen, and repent and weep before Him, and be comforted, and regirded, renew our strength for the race!

It is not by *one* act of faith, or *one* record of reproach to Him. that we enter into a knowledge of the mighty God of Jacob, but by considering his dealings and testing them by his Word. Such a review will always close with the renewed decision, "This God is my God for ever and ever; He shall be my guide even unto death."

Most of us can recall with joy the first visible seal upon service, the first soul given to our pleading, the first remembrance of forgotten vows, the first answer to prayer, after we have known the joy of calling Christ "Lord." They are landmarks of our spiritual life.

Such have been wrought out by the Holy Spirit, accepted, and blessed, and stand among the anointed pillars of our wilderness journey, anointed and blessed, as monuments of his promises and his faithfulness. Every book that has passed from my hand in faith and prayer has been such to me ; and over every one I would inscribe, " He is faithful that promised." I would refer to one perhaps better known in America than elsewhere, " Tell Jesus."

During a lengthened illness in England, I often mourned that I could not serve, where so many were needed, in the whitening harvest fields of the revival; not then perceiving that my place was assigned me, hedged up by my Father's hand of love, and marked out by the wisdom that cannot err. For the lack of recognizing this essential truth I have forfeited much blessing.

I was lodging in the country, in an ancient family house that stood in extensive grounds. The estate belonged to a minor, and was let until his majority to a family who apportioned the apartments for the reception of lodgers. The place had remained long in its primitive fashion. The shrubberies grew in wild luxuriance. There were trim box hedges, with peacocks and crosses formed from the Irish yew, which flanked the entrance, and were the only evidence of the special care and pride of the gardener who kept them in the formal fashion of days gone by. The grounds were surrounded by noble forest trees ; and in the centre, a knot of magnificent pines sheltered an old tennis lawn which was exposed to the early sunshine. At the extreme end, steps formed in the turf led to a bower of holly and arbutus as dense as the substantial peacocks of the entrance. It formed a welcome shelter for the birds in winter, and for myself in the summer.

When I first discovered this silent spot, I welcomed it as a loan from the Lord. where I could speak to Him, and commune with Him in freedom. Here many a trial I confided to Him, and He delivered me; many a sorrow, and He comforted me; and many an answered prayer is recorded that went up from the old tennis lawn.

I slowly recovered from my illness, and the first early summer day broke on me with unclouded beauty. Nothing seemed so alluring to me as to revisit the place from which I had been so long excluded, and spend my first morning of returning health in the bower beneath the pines.

I had often desired to write " Tell Jesus," as its recital had already wrought blessings by leading others to trust in the same living Saviour. Often I said, as I lay helplessly on my pillows, " If ever I am raised up again to use my pen, *I will write it.*" This morning the words rang in my memory like Jacob's vow. The gladness of heart I experienced was the natural effect of renewed health. I was longing to use the little strength granted me to revisit the old garden and breathe the delicious air. I stood at the bay-window and looked from the flower terrace near the house to the crowns of pine-trees in the centre of the shrubbery, bright in the morning sunlight, standing out against a sky of cloudless blue. Birds and bees were busy in the

garden-plot; it seemed a law of nature that I should
go forth and enjoy, too.

> But He knows best, we learn at last, —
> Oh, what a God is ours!
> He has better things for those He loves
> Than summer days and flowers.

I prepared to leave the house. Then began a conflict. Wherefore? Whether I would do my own will,
or the will of my Father which is 'in Heaven! I
argued, Would it not be a preparation for writing, if
I were strengthened by fresh air? Could I not do
both, — enjoy the garden for a few hours, and return to write? Was it not unwise to neglect such a
warm, bright morning? "Spare thyself!" so the enemy
argued. A strange gleam of joy thrilled my soul, as
I slowly received the idea that it would please the
Lord if I remained where I was, and wrote "Tell
Jesus." Peter said, "We have left *all* and followed
Thee." He left his father, his vessel, his nets, and his
fishing, and without the Lord's blessing they were of
little worth. But I had nothing to leave for Him but
my own will, and a sunny day on the old tennis lawn
without his blessing!

I said in my heart, "The sun will go down, and the
night will come, and I shall hardly remember the sunshine, but the words the Lord may lead me to write will
endure. Yes! Now Jesus of Nazareth — my Lord
and my King — was passing by, and my tiny bark must
take a *multitude* of fish. He said also to me, "I will
make you fishers of men."

Day by day, at intervals as I was able, I wrote at my book. He who had given me strength to begin it in his name, gave me promises of blessings and sealed them. When Christian brethren spoke contemptuously of my simple declaration of the life and strength I had found in telling Jesus my daily, nay, hourly needs, and all it had wrought in my new experience, I believed in the promise of special blessing that the Lord had given me, in my sainted friend's words; and I have lived to see it accomplished to the full. It has been for my weak hand to prepare the channels, but the Lord of Heaven and earth alone could fill them with living water.

Was I never tempted to disbelieve the promise the Lord had given me for my own consolation? Oh, yes! Many a conflict and many a temptation came to induce me to throw it aside, and to doubt if such an unfinished record could really be used of God. Some who read the proof criticised it. One urged me to omit my vision, as likely to hinder its usefulness; another prayed me to omit my little dressmaker's prayer for a pin; another, the blessing on the grapes, as making much of such an insignificant gift. But the Lord gave me strength to resist all such suggestions. I had none but the Lord to whom I could look for encouragement, — and it was enough! And when my heart sank, as sink it did sometimes, — not in looking forward to its possible failure, but in dread of finding that I had expected too much blessing, — He did not withdraw his tender support for my faithlessness. As Jesus sent to John the results of his ministry to prove that He was the Christ,

so the same gracious One met my sinking heart with
evidence that I had not expected too much, or trusted
Him too unreservedly. From many a bed of death He
sent me a sweet blessing of farewell from strength
derived from the simple pages; from many a sorrowful
heart came a song of gladness, gathered from *her* life
who, being dead, yet speaketh; and some of the
little seed was wafted into strange lands, none knew
how, and lived and bore fruit to Him whose eye could
alone follow it. From the gold fields of California,
from Africa and China and the islands of the seas, the
Lord was always showing forth his power and his love;
and when I was on my knees in prayer for America, for
a special blessing on the words from my weak head,
I rose up to take my first intimation that the Lord had
already heard my cry; and from one of the messengers
of the Most High — one of the friends the Lord has
given me — I received the answer to my prayer. A
letter from one whose name even I knew not, had
followed me week by week, and found me in Sicily at
the very moment that I most needed the wine of the
kingdom, — the voice of love and cheer. Yes! the
little bark had crossed the Atlantic chartered with
prayer, and had returned laden with blessing. Immediately after its publication it was made known to me
in what wondrous ways the Lord had brought about my
desires. The first intimation of his blessing was from
a Christian lady, who kept her night-watch by her
beloved niece, — a young lady laid down in the first
year of her marriage to suffer and die. In the silence
of midnight the invalid drew back the curtain and

inquired the name of the book with which she was so absorbed. She replied, —

" A new book : ' Tell Jesus.' "

" Read it aloud !" pleaded the invalid, " for I cannot sleep !" In vain the request was denied ; her entreaties overruled opposition, and in the silence of the sick-room, the book was read, and — blessed !

The following day the dying wife spoke to her husband of the rest that she had found in its simple pages, and begged him to send for many copies, to be given away in remembrance of her when she should be no more. In a few days the parcel arrived ; the books were placed on her bed, and she portioned them out with the names of all those who were to receive them. Then, asking for writing materials, she prepared to write the name or a word of love on each, — her husband's the first. Supported in his arms, her trembling fingers guided the pen in the last-written expression of her tenderness to him ; and it was completed in the act, the pen falling from her fingers, and her brief life's work was done for God — and for me !

According to her request, the books were given away to those who assembled at her funeral ; and the blank page in each had a language unwritten that went home to many hearts, for the hand that had given the gift lay cold and motionless in the coffin before them, and the lips were closed forever that bade them tell Jesus their griefs.

By this means this little seed was carried into many a home that would never have received it, but for the touching remembrance connected with the gift ; and this was one of the first visible answers for the circulation of the message committed to the Lord. A member of the family, quite unknown to me, desired that it should be communicated to me. I traced the hand of the Lord in thus strengthening me to serve and suffer, and enabling me to look to *Him*, and to Him only, to guide the frail bark committed to Him through tides and times, " on to the other side."

A little later, when obliged to tarry for a few hours in a strange place, in a time of rejection and discouragement, I took a copy, with a parcel of tracts, and went into the streets, seeking for some opening for distributing them. I was returning, quite unsuccessful, when my eye lighted on a cobbler, busily working in his stall, at an open door. I sat down by him on a vacant stool, and he listened, and we spoke together. Before I left I emptied my bag, to see what I could give him. Just then a country woman, on her way home, with her empty market-basket, stopped before us, and attentively considering the cover of the book on my knee, pointed to it, eagerly saying, —

" I know that book! I had it once, but my dear daughter begged it of me when she went to Australia, and I had not the heart to refuse her. On the voyage she lent it to many; and a young lady, an officer's wife, was converted through it; and it made my poor girl so happy! I am ashamed to want it back again."

And she wiped her eyes; and I wiped mine, and placed the book in her hand. Her unfeigned joy and thankfulness filled my heart with praise. I had gone forth, rejected by my own people, and in the country

woman, with her empty basket. I recognized the unconscious messenger of my gracious Lord, the Lord of
hosts; but " many such things are with Him."

Many prayers besides mine followed my little bark,
and it returned to them laden with blessing, proving
His faithfulness who says, " Call upon Me and I will
answer thee." " Cast thy bread upon the waters for
thou shalt find it after many days."

" Now then, O Lord God of Israel, let thy word be
verified which Thou hast spoken unto thy servant." (2
Chron. vi. 17.)

Amongst many dreams and visions that strengthened
me in sickness was the following : I seemed to stand
in a house open to the sky, built upon a rock. The
broad river flowed before me ; some parts were deep
waters, and some gentle streams on a shelving shore.
I inquired, " Why does a man's hand (that is, physical strength) cast with greater power and distance than
a woman's ?" for I had bread in my hand which I was
occupied in throwing on the waters. I cast a piece
feebly, and it fell on the verge of the water, so that the
wavelets could not carry it out. I threw again ; it fell
among a large flock of birds. One eagerly flew up and
then pounced upon it ; it broke into a hundred pieces,
and it fed many. I looked sadly at my bread that fell
too near the shore, and said mournfully, " All that is
lost ! " As I spoke, life came into the scattered mor-
sels, as if it had suddenly been transformed, and it made
its way unassisted by the waters into the midst of the
broad river. I saw a woman who walked on the water,
sometimes feeding birds, and sometimes working with

a spade : she looked neither to the right nor to the left ; she was not watching for results like me, but always at her work. A little while and I saw her *beneath* the water, and then waves, transparent even in the darkness. flowed over her head ; but she still kept faithfully at her work, never raising her head, but delving patiently in making deeper channels for the river. I saw that it was not sand she threw out. but heavy clay and loam. And I learned a lesson from the woman who worked by faith *on* the waters, and in patience under the waters. and I saw that the bread I cast forth with a feeble hand was not lost ; for how could I follow it on that wide river? And though much had been cast, the bread in my hand never diminished. " Not by might, nor by power, but by My Spirit, saith the Lord of Hosts." (Zech. iv. 6.) "Therefore trust thou in Him." (Job xxxv. 14.)

When we look back and trace the many lines of light that mark the Master's hand in withdrawing us from our purpose or leading us to profit, for myself I am overwhelmed by my own blindness and sinfulness and ingratitude. And yet, in considering his ways, I have been helped to wait and watch for the souls for whom *He* waits !

How many falls, how many tears, how many dangers and deliverances, how many disappointments and undeserved blessings, go to make up the sum of even a brief existence, — even before the days when light shone upon our ways. and before his holy name was an anchor to our soul !

Before I knew the Lord, my love for children led me

to desire to write for them and those who educated
them, keenly feeling my own need of sympathy in childhood, and still smarting from the loveless surroundings
of a delicate organization and uncomprehended mind.
I had a firm conviction that happiness was not to be
found in the world with the miserable elements around
me ; but the way of escape into the haven of rest I
knew not, and no one ever set it before me. But at all
events I thought I would try and lay before others the
advantage of early training, evil and good, and this I
strove to develop in a narrative. Long and diligently
I worked at my book. I wrote it and rewrote it. It
consisted of eight chapters. It was perhaps the best
arranged of any of my books. I had great power of
application. I had not known so much of the sick-
nesses and sorrows that enfeeble the willing hand, and
a wearied mind.

At last it was finished, and now I must seek a suitable publisher. But how was this to be effected? It
was mentioned and afterwards placed in the hands of
the editor of a semi-religious periodical, and an offer
was made to me for it, to be used as a serial.

This was something for a nameless author, but it did
not satisfy me, so I declined it. My ambition was to
see my book stand alone. In this i must have been
unconsciously guided, for it was an open door for my
future publications.

One day after much deliberation (of prayer for guidance I knew nothing), I took it to Mr. Nesbit, of
Berners Street, London. I had a great respect for
him, because he sold good books. His shop seemed a

treasure-house of precious things to me, though I knew
not their value. I at once decided that was the place
for my book.

Accordingly, one gloomy afternoon in November, I
set off to Berners Street, elated with the hope that I
should soon see the completion of my desire.

I sent in my manuscript and a note asking for an interview. I waited impatiently what appeared a long
time before I received any attention. At last I was
ushered into the comfortable private room of the kind
old Scotchman. My manuscript lay open before him
on the table. He had evidently read enough of it to see
plainly that I knew nothing of the way of salvation, —
nothing of the priceless gift of God's sinless Son ; and
with the desire to point others to eternal things, I knew
nothing whatever about them myself. He led me to
speak of myself, of my motherless childhood, my loneliness, and my craving to live for a purpose. More
than once he brushed away the tears that filled his eyes.
He excused himself by saying that I reminded him
strangely of a beloved friend who was now no more.
And then the kind old man inquired with a gentle
voice, —

" But why do you call your book ' The Godmother ' ?
there is no such word in the book of *God* as ' godmother.' "

" That may be," I replied readily, remembering only
the catechism of the Church of England as my au-
thority ; " but there are many good institutions not
written in the Bible, and this is a very useful one."

" How so ? " he inquired, with a smile at my eager
defence of my title.

For the first time my mind was aroused to *think* of what I had undertaken to prove ; for I had never felt clear as to the value of the promises and vows made for me at my baptism, by my sponsors, which had never been fulfilled. Suddenly light seemed breaking over a subject that had often perplexed me. However, I felt I must defend the position I had taken, and replied, —

" When the father and mother die, then the real office of the godmother is to take care of and give good instruction to the child for whose well-being she has made herself responsible."

There was a pause ; he shook his head. There was something sad, almost solemn in his voice, as slowly and impressively he replied. —

" Nay, when my father and my mother forsake me, *then* the LORD taketh me up ! "

The kind old man took my hand with an expression of such kindly interest as made me forgive him for carefully packing up my manuscript, and said, " My dear child, God has given you a talent. I feel assured that some day you will know these things better, and lay yourself and your talent on his altar ; then come to me, and *I will publish your book.*"

He accompanied me to the shop, and called for one tract after another, which he prayed me to accept and read ; which I never did, except one of Newton's hymns appended as a leaflet to one of them, which took my ear and my heart in a strange way and never left it again,— most likely never will ! Nor did I recognize until years afterwards the heavenly message therein enfolded.

" I asked the Lord that I might grow
   In faith and love, and every grace,
Might more of his salvation know,
   And seek more earnestly his face.
'T was He who taught me thus to pray,
And He I know has answered prayer,
But it has been in such a way
   As almost drove me to despair.

" I thought that in some favored hour,
   At once He 'd grant me my request,
And with his love's constraining power
   Subdue the sin and give me rest.

   .   .   .   .

" These inward trials I employ,
   From self and pride to set thee free,
That thou may'st lose thy earthly joy,
   And find thy only rest in Me."

Little did I think those prophetic verses stood forth as my ordained experience, and that before I should again cross that threshold I must first pass through the flood and the furnace, and find Jesus in the one, — and One like unto the Son of God in the other!

Not in the quiet room of the kind and sympathizing Christian veteran was I to enter into the light that revealed my need of a Saviour. I was to learn that all my work was " as an oak whose leaf fadeth, and as a garden that hath no water"; that I was bound in the grave-clothes, the captive of death, and no man cared for my soul.

It was a brief interview, and the gloomy afternoon had changed to a dark night, as I entered the house I had left with such bright hopes; and yet, perhaps, though only the eye of God beheld it, the first line of light trembled on the chaos of darkness in which I existed I was deeply struck with the sympathy of the kind old man unlike any one I had then seen.

I marvelled (long afterwards) that the dear old Scotchman did not set forth the way of salvation to me, and tell me I was a poor lost sinner. I think it would have come with power from his lips. It was not so ordained. " My time is not yet; your time is always ready."

I confess I was discouraged by my expedition to Berners Street. I had yet to learn that natural religion without change of heart is but Cain's sacrifice, and is but a cradle to rock the soul to slumber for perdition. I was to learn the plague of my own heart, and why the Son of God became also the son of man, to suffer and to die for lost sinners, such as I.

But my " Godmother " was still at hand; I could not add to it, neither could I take from it, for I had no more light. so the book and its writer must still sit in darkness and the shadow of death. I regarded my offspring with a little less affection, and I looked more scrutinizingly at the Church of England catechism to defend my position, but in vain; but I did not like my labor to be lost.

A lady of influence offered me an introduction to another publisher, and drove me to the house in her carriage. I was received with great courtesy, most likely in consequence. The principal of the firm promised to consider my manuscript and let me have his decision in a few days. Weeks went by ; at last I received a polite letter, regretting that they could not accept it,— that such a book would be unexpected from their house, — but advising me still to publish it : he had found great interest in the story, and had sat up till midnight to finish it. As I laid down the letter, I thought that publishers were very pleasant people after all. — This was my first book ! — Again my " Godmother " was on my hands. I was not to be daunted. Once more an introduction was given me to a High Church publisher, who seemed inclined to take it. He suggested alterations and improvements and additions, and went so far as to print off a sheet, to show me the type and the paper and the style, and make arrangements for the quantity. So I saw the book which was to do so much in educating sponsors and children, really a chapter in print.

At this epoch I was suddenly called away from London. I had abruptly to close the business, and all interest in the " Godmother " vanished. It was all the Lord's tender care, all a Father's love, though my blind eyes saw only chance and change. My manuscript lay with other sketches and poems packed up in a portmanteau,— the best place for it, until it was called forth for the Lord's purpose.

I was in the world and of the world (save that I never felt any of the peace or pleasure that others seemed to find), and sought in form and ceremonial worship to weigh against the sins and follies and stupid allurements that bind the soul in chains of iron. Many a sigh went up for better things. I met with Christiaus very rarely. They never addressed me on the way of salvation, or exhibited any sympathy, or told me of the joy of their hope and whence they drew it. Yet they blamed me for having no lot or portion with them. And others who were sincere, and might have helped me, thought it useless speaking to one so far away. Yet often I was in despair to think that their Saviour whom I admired was not my Saviour.

Artistically adorned churches, early, intoned services, lighted altars, all failed to bring light to my dark soul, — and I thank God that it was so. Also from my own desert solitude I learned to pity others, and not judge the worldling too far off for the voice of love or rebuke, — too far, in fact, for the Lord's hand to reach We pretend to fathom the desires of a heart whose depth of misery and longing for Him is seen by Himself only; nay, who may be sighing after the only One who can give rest to the weary and heavy-laden.

Other ambitions and other follies filled my life; my " Godmother" was forgotten. I felt I had the power of writing, so I wrote. I did not shrink from application; I had no mercenary spirit. I needed an aim. We can only teach what we know, and I knew only what I saw. Several of my manuscripts I kept by me, from time to time improving and altering them, secure that some day they would be stepping-stones to the slumbering ambition which I bless my gracious Lord He never allowed to spring into life. Some were published, but I never felt any gratification in seeing them in print, as I observed others had. Those unpublished were of more value; they were hidden treasures, because more pains had been expended on their preparation. In all these items there was the hand of Him who had his eye of love on me, restraining the fruition of my vain thoughts, and guiding me though I knew it not.

Years went on. Sorrows and trials, best calculated to break the world's power over me, were making in the desert a highway for my God   Yes; I had in a way found what I supposed Mr Nisbet meant. I longed to hear his voice again, to remind him of his prophecy and his promise, that I now dared to claim. I had brought him a book, and he would publish it, as he said he would. And if he had prayed for the foolish, ignorant, self-sufficient creature (as doubtless he had) in years gone by, he might trace some fruit of his prayers, as he had done in the case of Captain Trotter.*

The day after I arrived in London I went to the Presbyterian church in Regent Square, of which church Mr. Nisbet was an elder, greatly honored and loved.

An unusual crowd attended, and a strange solemnity marked the service. Dr. Hamilton brought his sermon

---

* Captain Trotter bought some books in Berners Street, and was about to write his address, when Mr. Nisbet told him he knew it well ; adding, "I have prayed for you ever since you were as high as my table. You and your sister had a young nursery governess, who felt sadly alone in this great metropolis. She was a dear child of God, and came to me to tell me of her concern for the souls of her little pupils. She was cast down by the charge. I felt for her, comforted her, and she was strengthened ; and every Saturday she came to my house, and together we prayed for your salvation and that of your sister, and I have lived to see the fruit which we desired."

to an abrupt termination, and in deep emotion appealed
to his hearers, who knew the loss he had sustained, to
uphold him with their prayers and sympathy. The congregation separated silently, noiselessly. As I passed
the door I inquired of the old verger why the people
were so sad. He replied, " Do you not know that Mr.
Nisbet died last night?"

A pang went through my heart, as if I had lost a
friend. He was the only Christian to whom I could
look at that moment, to whom I turned for help and
encouragement, — and he was gone! In a moment the
past came back, as I stood before the kind old man as
he bade me lay myself and my talents on the altar of the
everlasting Father. I had striven to do so now, —
how feebly, how ignorantly, He knew; how dimly, yet I
apprehended the blessed truth of salvation! and he
who would have rejoiced was gone. I could not publish my poems without his name on the title-page ; but I
learned even by that, I was walking in sentiment, not in
grace. But the Lord God Omnipotent reigneth.

But my " Godmother," — what of it? I consulted with
a friend who knew its history, and that of my other
writings, and I was advised to remodel this and others
according to the light that had been given me. Contrary to my own judgment, I examined it for this
purpose, and I promised to go through it with this end
in view.

I pondered over it, and desired to do the Lord's will ;
but it seemed to me putting new wine into old bottles,
and that was foolishness. I had found Him of whom
the prophets spoke ; I scarcely hoped to serve Him,

but I longed to testify of his grace, and go home and rest with Him forever.

I took my "Godmother" from its hiding-place of years. The time had come when the Lord had need of it. I gathered together all that on which I had spent my precious time for that which was not bread, and my labor on that which had not satisfied me, — weary now of its very vanity. I longed to leave all and follow Jesus, little comprehending what to leave *all* included. It was a solemn time to me. I seemed to stand alone with God. Many a thing is laid on the altar for acceptance, and the heart that lays it there receives it back again ; but this was to be consumed. I deliberately tore up chapter after chapter and laid it on the smouldering embers. Once only I paused, when, like Judas, the thought struck me they might have been sold for much and given to the poor. The God of the whole earth, who accepts the meanest offering of his children, accepted mine. A calm persuasion that I was doing his will came over me with a power I had never felt before. Other works followed ; some in print, some in proof, and some of the hidden treasures on which I had so often labored. It was one of those transactions between the soul and God which sometimes catches a gleam of that which shall be ; faint and evanescent it may be, yet a foreshadowing of that which *shall* come hereafter. *Jesus only.* What is anything worth but to tell of the Saviour of sinners, the Friend that sticketh closer than a brother, — to proclaim to those who knew Him not, of his love and his beauty and his grace? For this I consecrated my life in that hour. How little have I fulfilled the promise! but like Jacob. I return to Bethel, with his Bethel promise. I am unfaithful, but He is faithful! What He has said, that will He do ; and what He has promised, that will He perform!

CHAPTER II.

PRAYER.

" He will be very gracious unto thee at the voice of thy cry; when He shall hear it, He will answer thee." — Is. xxx. 19.

" The multitude wondered, when they saw the dumb to speak, the maimed to be whole, the lame to walk, and the blind to see : and they glorified the God of Israel." — Matt. xv. 31.

" Blessed is the man that heareth me, *watching* daily at my gates, *waiting at the posts of my doors!* " Prov. viii. 34.

 DYING Christian gazed in tender love upon her nine children surrounding her bed; some were hopefully converted, and some still far from God.

" My children ! " she said, as the mother-love beamed in her face, already shadowed by the angel of death, — " my children ! I have not a thousand pounds to leave you, but I have thousands of prayers laid up for you before the Lord."

" God is not mocked : for whatsoever a man soweth, that shall he also reap " She looked on from the things which are seen, to the things which are not seen and are eternal !

" Prove me herewith," remains for us ; and if not by sight, then by faith, we shall *see* the glory of God.

Why do we slight his Fatherly injunction, when our only help is in the living God? Why do we distrust and thus cast dishonor on the Holy One of Israel, the Great I AM? " Call upon Me." He repeats ; " ask," " seek," " knock." Why are we listless, as if it were of no use to ask and seek and knock? Why are we mourning over our wretchedness, and little grace, when He longs to give abundantly, and cries, " Open thy mouth wide, and I will fill it " ?

Prayer is a great fact. Men may philosophize, argue, scorn and deny its efficacy : but there it stands with its rich promises in the covenant of grace ; it glows like a pillar of light in our own lives and in the lives of others. It is a trophy of the Saviour's triumph (John xvi. 24), vested in the hand and heart of the believer, whose strength is in the Lord Jesus Christ, the power of God, and the wisdom of God.

Why do we see so little result from this hallowed power committed to a child of the dust, an heir of glory, when its exercise involves untold influences?

Wonderful to reply, — from the incredulity of Christians, to whom have been allotted the positions of prince and priest (Peter ii. 9) ; to whom has been intrusted the golden key of the treasury of heaven (John xv. 7), with a thousand promises to encourage the timid soul to enter into the presence chamber with his petition. Yet with aching heart he often stands without, not knowing if the thing he desires is according to the mind of God, not asking for spiritual intelligence, which would strengthen him to ask and receive. " The Lord is at hand. Be careful for nothing ; but in *everything* by prayer and supplication with thanksgiving let your requests be made known unto God. And the peace of God, which passeth all understanding, shall keep your hearts and minds through Christ Jesus." (Phil. iv. 5. 6, 7.) The faith that pleads must wait in faith ; for He who caused the east wind to blow, by his power can bring the south wind.

Perhaps the suppliant is weary of waiting ; he has cried once, twice, thrice, to the Lord, and then, faint-hearted and afraid, the hands become slack, as if it were in vain to wait upon the Lord God any longer (2 Kings xiii. 9). To receive the fulness of his request he should have knocked six, seven, nay, seventy times, if need be ; knocked according to his need, and the faithfulness of Him to whom he had made known his request. "For Christ is not entered into the holy places made with hands. which are the figures of the true ; but into heaven itself, now to appear in the presence of God for us." (Heb. ix. 24.)

Persevering prayer is the fruit of faith and patience. If we consider God's ways with us aforetime, we shall not be discouraged when the answer tarries, to teach us that this very perseverance is to nourish the hidden life. "But if we hope for that we see not, then do we with patience wait for it." (Rom. viii. 25.)

We are prone to dwell on the external trials of our natural life, as if a citizen of heaven were to be exempt from them, forgetting that we are appointed thereunto. (1 Thes. iii.) By the exercise of faith which they involve, we are led to realize the position of the worshipper within the veil, where the Great High-Priest stands to plead for and to judge his people. (Is. iii. 13.)

We cannot fathom God's purposes ; but we may and should seek Him in the circumstances that so often rise like battlements against us, in the way of service and testimony into which we have been guided by Him. " Now the just shall live by faith : but if any man draw back, my soul shall have no pleasure in him." (Heb. x. 38.)

Patience (the least sought and least cultivated fruit of the Holy Spirit) manifests by its presence that the soil that the husbandman is tilling is neither barren nor unfruitful. Let any one gather up the injunctions and promises linked with this heavenly grace, and he will assuredly more ardently desire the quiet confidence that springs from the root of faith ; for " the trying of your faith worketh patience." (James.) And " by faith and patience we inherit the promises."

How shall we define prayer? Where shall we limit it? As to where it begins or where it ends, what is too high or what is too mean for a subject of prayer? If the aspirations after a deeper knowledge of Christ Himself be prayer ; if all the desires for the glory of God, enfolded in our longings for others to partake in the treasures hid in Jesus, be prayer ; if the yearning to serve Him better in his sanctuary, and the craving of the soul for deeper, closer, more intimate communion with Him be prayer, — then prayer is the most important of all services, the most heavenly of all occupations, the truest preparation for the endless life. The service here may be unseen of men save by its results ; yet it is a perpetual testimony by its influence, and a source of marvel to principalities and powers, of the mystery of the Cross : for the Great Adversary watches for the soul that becomes strange to the mercy-seat, and

> "Trembles when he sees
> The weakest saint upon his knees."

The incredulity of *Christians* as to the efficacy and necessity of prayer is one of the marvels of this age of religious ceremonial. Any one may gain a hearing with idle Christians ; men will listen to sermons or addresses by the hour, who will not spend the same time alone before the mercy-seat themselves. The object of the Enemy is to prevent this. If no other snare succeeds, he will fill the mind with abstruse questions, that have no bearing on salvation, no influence to induce continual communion with the Lord ; or he will weary the body with what he suggests is work for the Lord, but which is nothing more than nature's energy, so that the jaded body, acting on the nerves, throws the shadow of despondency on its heavenly enjoyment of prayer and praise. This is Satan's masterpiece. Then, when prayer is no longer possible, the Enemy comes down upon the sad, bewildered heart, taunting it with remembered transgressions, drawing the unwary foot to Sinai. Thus precious hours, which might have been records of the grace and goodness and glory of God, are swallowed up in self-retrospection. For the God that Satan sets before us is an austere master, — a jealous God, a righteous and implacable judge ; and beneath the terrors of the law, we forget that the Father gave his beloved Son to die for one who now cries in despairing grief, as if there were no God in Zion, "The Lord hath forsaken me, and my God hath forgotten me." Nay, hath not He declared in ancient days, and does He not repeat to-day, "Can a woman forget her sucking child, that she should not have compassion on the son of her womb? yea, they may forget, yet will I not forget thee. Behold, I have graven thee upon the palms of my hands."

"When the enemy shall come in like a flood, the Spirit of the Lord shall lift up a standard against him."

In one of my city sojourns I met a dear, aged missionary, who for many years had served the Lord in the burning clime of Africa. Toil and sickness had incapacitated her for further service in the mission field, and she had returned to await the Lord's home call in the land of her birth. She was a prayerful and a praiseful Christian, and great was my enjoyment to commune with her. She longed for and eagerly sought some quiet country retreat, where she could enjoy repose in her latter days. I left the city where we had met, never expecting to see her again on earth.

Two years or more afterwards I returned to the same neighborhood, where friends I had recently made invited me to accompany them into the country, where they had business to transact, and proposed leaving me for a few hours on the outskirts of the village, at a house that received a few inmates for change of air, free of rent charge; and amongst them, at present, was a missionary whom they thought I should like to know. Her name was unknown; but I had no doubt of finding,

to my infinite refreshment, my unforgotten sister in the .
Lord.

The carriage left me at the garden gate, and I loi-
tered in the old-fashioned garden among the fragrant
herbs and blooming flowers, in the glowing sun of an
autumn afternoon. The fruit trees were bending with
their luxuriant burdens, and the vine trellis formed a
shadowed walk to the ancient well. As I walked
slowly along the paved terrace to the house, I rejoiced
in the peaceable habitation and quiet resting-place which
God's dear servant had found at last.

I entered, and the first door at which I knocked was
that of her of whom I was in search. It was a large,
pleasant chamber, with two aspects : one looking on
the garden, the other on the whitening harvest fields,
banked by pine-covered hills, which, with the scattered
villages, made a cheerful prospect.

All was bright except the face of the dear inmate :
her pale and haggard countenance betokened the distress within ; but when, with an exclamation of delight,
she recognized her visitor, the shadows passed away,
and praise (which was the prominent feature of her
spiritual life) burst forth anew.

Oh, how she thanked the Lord for guiding me *there*
first! Then, holding my hands in her own, as if she
feared to lose me, she told over the conflicts which had
been her portion since she entered that quiet abode, —
deeper and sharper this week than before. The pleasant retreat and the sweet country stillness only seemed
to have formed a broader battle-field for the Enemy to
assault her ; and she, who had lived and taught the

sweet liberty of love, was being ground down under the terror of the law.

The sword of the Spirit seemed to fail in her faltering hand; Satan stood by to accuse, continuously reading over her sins to her sinking heart: yet that feeble woman's cry was not unheard, though *He* who could have ended the conflict would triumph again in his weak but precious trophy.

Like a trumpet voice rang through her prostrate soul, " Point him to Calvary." The blood of Jesus Christ cleanseth from all sin.

Like a benighted traveller who has watched for the faint streak of dawn in the east, hope rose within her; the God of her hope was at hand: and with a power that set her free she exclaimed, —

" Yes! all these sins have I committed, and many more that thou knowest not. Go! behold them at Calvary,"

" And there was a great calm." Not for long could she say, " It is peace "; in a few days the conflict was renewed. The same Enemy who met our Divine Forerunner in the wilderness, who carried Him to the pinnacle of the Temple in the Holy City, who tempted Him on the mountain, was now again to prove the truth of the written Word. The heel of the man should bruise the serpent's head. (Gen. iii. 15.)

One word, only one, responded to the fierce accusations of Satan : "Golgotha." It was enough : " By every word that proceedeth out of the mouth of God shall man live!" The mighty debt was thus paid by the mighty love that poured out the blood (which is the

Life) for the sinner. Worn in body, sleepless, exhausted, as one whom the Evil One had rent, for the third time the conflict was renewed; when, surely sent of God, I crossed the threshold, and at the cry of joy and praise that welcomed me as such, the devil departed " for a season."

The anguish passed from the wan, careworn face, and while we talked together of all these things that had happened, Jesus Himself drew nigh, and our hearts burned within us. She received me as one sent of Him who once, "sorrowful and very heavy," in His own lone night-watch in the garden, knew how sweet is human sympathy, which *He* lacked for our sakes, that He might enter into all our sorrows as the " Man of Sorrows," feel our loneliness by his own desolation, and, tempted even as we are, yet without sin, become acquainted with all our griefs.

How often do we think that certain positions would kindle our cold hearts to worship more acceptably the God of grace; that if we were otherwhere than in the place He had chosen for us, we should serve Him more ardently and worship Him more fervently! Emotional delight in the Creator of this beautiful earth is not enduring. The roaring cataract in the morning sunshine, the starry heavens, or the lofty mountains may elevate the mind for a time, but clouds of earth will obscure the beauty; but the eye of faith, resting on Jesus only, will find a glory in the meanest thing that we can bring to his feet. He who has chosen our habitation for us, knows the trials and service which belong to it; and in his light we shall see light,

and the meanest service will thus become a hallowed
offering.

"Herein is my Father glorified, that ye bear much
fruit ; so shall ye be my disciples." When the vintage
is over, it will matter little if the fruit ripened on a barren hill or on a fruitful plain, on a cottage trellis or an
orchard bower, save in the lesson of its life, so full of
instruction to those who need the care of the Heavenly
husbandman over the vine of his right-hand plant-
ing.

To believe in the unchanging love of God is one of
the weapons of the warfare of faith, more especially
needful for persevering prayer. "Blessed are all they
that wait for Him." The believer will hold every
petition on the basis of subjection : "If it be *Thy* will, —
Thy will be done." If it is granted palpably, we may
see that what we have desired is given ; but it may be
given although the form of the prayer is denied. Anyway
there is an answer from the Lord ; for if it is not given,
He answers still, "It is not for my glory ; it is not
well, my child"(1 John v. 14, 15). The mighty transaction involved in that mysterious vigil of Gethsemane,
"If it be *possible, let this cup pass fr m me,*" was the
most perfect form of subject prayer, from the most
perfect servant. For the glory of our redemption, it
was *not* possible. And for us to-day there are requests
that, however expedient to our view, yet contain in
themselves that which we know not, and involve consequences hidden from all but that All-seeing Eye that
beholds the end from the beginning. To grant it
would be to detract from that which is always nearest

to the heart of the believer, — the glory of the Father, the prosperity of his own soul !

If he answers not at once, it may be to increase the faith of the suppliant. whose former petition may have been, " Increase my faith." The Holy Spirit in that silence may bring to mind the gracious character of the God with whom we have to plead. We have expected the answer in some form of our own imagery, — any way rather than in patient waiting ; or the delay may be to bring in a greater amount of blessing. " Unless ye see signs and marvels ye will not believe."

Again, one complains of unanswered prayer. It may be that you have asked for deeper knowledge of *Himself*, and special grace you needed, and there comes a flood of trials, each one sharper than the last ; and when *He* whom we desire to know better is hidden from our eyes, it is hard to believe that faith is thus being strengthened for the " afterwards " of the coming harvest. " All things work together for good to them that love God." Be patient ! they are often a long time working together, but God has said it, and it must be so as He has said ; " for the word of the Lord is right, and all his works are done in truth." (Ps. xxxiii. 4.)

If we are often at the Throne of Grace, we are in the line of gracious things, and some of them must be ours.

There are many eloquent prayers that have no real need expressed, no real desire of the heart for that which our lips utter, — because it seemed a duty to pray for it. Often we are taught this by some urgent necessity, which drives us to our knees with " Lord, help, or

I perish," which brings the Lord now as ever to help and save.

I remember a time of coldness and deadness of heart. I could not trace whence it sprang, but it was sufficient that I lost the joy of carrying the burdens laid on me to the only One who could help. So my service was a joyless one, and I missed the blessing of sharing my days' changing lights and shadows with Him who had been my strength and my shield. I could not remain long in such a dreary land. But how was I to attain anything better? *Attain*, indeed! I possessed nothing apart from *Him*. My need was my plea, and very faintly pleaded. I could only cast my cold, lifeless heart on Him who had first given it life, and entreat Him quickly to enliven it.

It was the eve of my departure from London, under circumstances that necessitated my taking a certain train. I went to pay a farewell visit to a friend near Kensington Gardens, and took a Park chaise in the evening for my return. The chaise-man carelessly struck the wheel against the trunk of a tree, and it broke. I escaped unhurt, but my leather bag with its contents lay scattered in the long grass. We gathered the articles together as well as the deepening twilight would allow, not without some distrustful fears on my part that some might be missing.

Had I been as in days past, I should have sought the Lord before I left the spot, that nothing should be lost; but I contented myself with rejoicing that I had sustained no bodily injury, and returned to my lodging to make preparation for my next day's journey.

But my keys! where were they? Not one or two, but all! Everything was locked, from my portmanteau to my writing-case. I sought them in my bag. I searched every pocket. I felt assured that they were there. I searched in vain. No keys!

Then began to roll over me the helpless misery of one who could not say in the old familiar security of sympathy and love, "Help, Lord!" Thus passed hours in the search; but now with my great need came forth a cry of distress to the very-present God. The icy cobweb that seemed to have entwined my heart was broken, and I had cast my care on Him. But my keys were not seen. Worn out in body, and weary in mind, I threw myself on my bed; and prayed the Lord for sleep, to prepare me for my journey, and in *faith* asked Him to send me my lost keys when I awoke, for He could see them.

I slept a deep sleep, and when I awoke it was made known to me, as distinctly as I have often received such communications, that the lost keys were in the bag. For a moment I feared a delusion: I had so carefully searched it I argued that if there I must have found them; but the word came, "Their eyes were holden," and I followed blindly. Within the thick leather lining of the bag the keys were closely thrust, from the force with which the chaise had fallen. Ah! then I knew why my keys were lost! and my soul sprang up like a lark in the summer sky with its song of praise, and I praised Him for the prayer — feebly prayed, but still the prayer of faith, trusting in Him alone — for grace for my graceless heart. He had led me by the right way to learn another lesson of His love.

> "Like dew on the drooping plant,
>   Like the prisoned bird set free,
> Like summer after the winter's day,
>   Was his sweet smile on me.
> As the sunshine's golden glow
>   On the ruddy, vine-clad hill,
> Brightens the pebbles of the brook,
>   'T is his same sunshine still.
>
> "It floods the ocean's breast,
>   Spreads o'er the flowery mead,
> Kisses the tall pine's verdant crest,
>   And bathes the river's reed.
> Naught is too mean, too low,
>   For God to cheer and bless;
> His storm and sun, his drought and dew,
>   Shall bring forth fruitfulness."

When we marvel why Israel did *not* believe the message of the Lord by Moses, a message so full of promise and power, we forget our own unbelief. Though He has done so many miracles before us, how little do we expect Him to do all He has promised, all we desire, all He is able! Yet the least groan of his people is felt by Him, and his loving heart is continually moved by the sighs and tears of his afflicted ones.

The heart of Israel was bowed down under an increased and overwhelming burden, and they hearkened not, from anguish of heart and cruel bondage. The Lord, merciful and gracious, does not reproach them for their murmurings, for at that time they had

had no experience of his power and his faithfulness ; but
pitifully declares, " I have heard the groaning of the
children of Israel, whom the Egyptians keep in bondage :
and I have remembered my covenant." He is the
same to-day and forever.

When Hezekiah wept sore and prayed for life, the
Lord answers him, " I have heard thy prayer, I have
seen thy *tears*, I will heal thee." (2 Kings.) He will
be very gracious at the voice of *your* cry ; when He
hears He will answer *you*. When have you sought his
face in vain? Everywhere in his holy Word we trace
his grace and goodness to those whom He had delivered,
who had yet provoked Him by their counsel, and were
brought low for their iniquity ; nevertheless He regarded
their affliction when He heard their cry, and He remembered for them his covenant, and repented according to
the multitude of His mercies. (Ps. cv.)

He is ever waiting to be gracious, delighting in
mercy, taking pleasure in the prosperity of his servants.

When David tuned his harp to tell of the goodness
of the Lord to the unthankful and rebellious, he
declared Him " nigh to all that call upon Him in *truth*.
He will fulfil the desire of them that fear Him : He
also will hear their cry, and will save them." David,
remembering the catalogue of mercies shown to the
people of Israel, could tell out of his own rich experience, " In *my* distress I cried unto the Lord, and He
heard *me*." (Ps. cxxi.) If you place yourself in the
position of blessing, you must be blest. If you have
sought light, help, counsel, — believe, and you shall

have it. But if we leave the Throne of Grace, and the means of grace, with the natural satisfaction that we have done a good work, rather than that we have received, — whether it be counsel, guidance, reproof, or whatsoever we needed, — we shall find that we have lost, not gained; lost our time, our strength, and often, in the end, our peace. We are there to receive, out of that fulness that waits to give. When we remember that every prayer is heard and considered, we shall be often led to scrutinize the form of our petitions, and what prayer really is. It is the heart's desire that rests on Almighty love to grant, — on Omnipotence alone to give.

Prayer may have been eloquent, yet have had no real need expressed, and therefore have seen no practical result. The momentary satisfaction of having spoken words with ease and fluency will fade away as the petitioner returns into more practical life; and instead of watching unto prayer, and working out by heavenly wisdom what the lips requested, the momentary content of having performed a duty will have passed as the morning cloud, and as the early dew it goeth away.

The need of our daily extremities to bring us face to face with Omnipotence will be more and more evident to those who seek to walk intelligently with the Lord. If the soul would grow in knowledge of Him, it must be constantly at the Source of Life. If we would *know* the Lord God Almighty, who brought us out of the land of Egypt, we must wait on Him to reveal Himself to us, and not set the form and manner of that revelation in

our reason or imagination. "Then shalt thou understand the fear of the Lord, and find the knowledge of
God. For the Lord giveth wisdom : out of his mouth
cometh knowledge and understanding. He layeth up
sound wisdom for the righteous : he is a buckler to
them that walk uprightly. He preserveth the way of
His saints." (Prov. ii. 5–8.) Surely He is more ready
to give than we to receive. Wherefore, then, should
there be any doubt that the grace ordained shall be
given? Will He withhold one good thing from his waiting people, who only rely on his faithfulness for blessing? He ever liveth to make intercession for us ; and
while the tempted, troubled heart sinks in its effort to
rise to God, like a dove beaten in a storm, there
sounds through the heavenly atmosphere, could we but
catch the echo, "*I have prayed for thee.*" Let all the
earth keep silence before Him.

There is no promise as to the time or manner in
which prayer is to be answered. He has said, "Call
upon Me and I will answer thee." We cannot count
the cost, nor measure that which has no measure,—
the love and power of God in granting   Well may He
have said to the disciples who would partake of his cup,
"Ye know not what ye ask "

I was in prayer with a dear friend in the Lord, and
I trembled at her almost passionate supplication that
God would renew his work in her soul and give her of
the grace she sought, at any cost. While I knelt there
I felt the Lord had heard, and my soul received a fore-
taste of the cross that was on its way, unseen by human
eyes, to bring an answer she little looked for. Not only

that day, but many times, I was drawn to the feet of the Lord in anguish of spirit for her, without knowing wherefore.

I communicated to her something of what I felt; but the transmission of this interior sensibility, depending on sympathy, cannot be communicated. But I wrote to her on the subject. She answered that there was nothing to account for it, and when I saw her again she was full of active service for the Lord. The shadow on my soul had not reached *her.* She dwelt on the success of much she was engaged in, believing it an answer to her prayer, and only slightly glancing at my trouble for her as imaginative.

Suddenly there swept over her the deepest trial of her life. An only and beloved sister, the partner in her work, the companion of her joys and sorrows. was smitten down under circumstances the most appalling; and the soul which had been crying for a knowledge of God's will and grace at any cost could not read, through the anguish of a broken heart, the answer to the prayer which had not counted the cost. Oh, well might the Holy One, whose eye seeth every secret thing, and beholds the future we could not look upon and live, say, " Ye know not what ye ask "

Although at a long distance from them, and knowing nothing of the close of her earthly life, it was given me to share the grief of the mourner in a peculiar manner, and it was also given me to partake yet more remarkably of the joy of the departing one.

I was on the eve of a journey. I awoke from a brief, troubled slumber, with the words impressed on my mind, " This day ye shall cross over the Jordan " ; and again, " When ye are come to the brink of the waters of Jordan, ye shall stand still in Jordan." All day long I seemed to feel death near me, and through my long railway journey I expected some accident for which I had been prepared.

I arrived at my destination late in the afternoon, and retired early to my room, but not to sleep. Hour by hour tolled forth from the old tower near the house, as if waiting for I knew not what. But this spiritual sense of the overshadowing of the presence of the Holy One deepened ; and as it deepened, I marvelled if indeed I was about to cross the boundary into my home of many mansions.

Then rang through my soul, distinct and clear, " At midnight I will arise and give thanks." Accordingly, when the midnight hour sounded forth from the belfry, I arose to praise.

From that hour until dawn, there was given me such a reality of bliss unutterable and full of glory, such a consciousness of angelic guardianship, such depths of peace and rest and freedom, as I have seldom or never known except in slumber. This continued until the morning had dawned. It was a watch-night indeed ! Even so might Elisha have felt as Elijah mounted his fiery chariot and passed from the clouds of earth into the glorious city of his God !

Surely, by the wondrous law of compensation, I had tasted of the shadow of death, that I might also realize something of that heavenly journey, — not by hearsay, but experimentally tell of those joys reserved

for the children of the Kingdom, the ransomed heirs
of glory.

At six o'clock the freed spirit had departed. The
long, fatiguing journey, my lonely dwelling-place, the
pallid hours of sorrow and pain, all were as nothing.
The very air of heaven seemed to have renewed my
strength, and deep, silent peace followed the hour when
the weary one passed from the furnace into the presence
of the King. I turned to my Bible for a text, and my
eyes fell on Rev. xxii. 6. The following day brought
a brief note from her sister, giving me the hour of her
departure, and commencing with the word "*Praise.*"

It may be asked, why was this joy and sorrow given
me to share so acutely, and in such a peculiar way?
Ah! we know not why, but " many such things are
with Him." Yet He can reveal even this unto us.
What we know not now we shall know hereafter " He
revealeth the deep and secret things : He knoweth what
is in the darkness, and the light dwelleth with Him."
(Dan. ii. 22.)

Perhaps the action of the Spirit through our prayers
on the heart of another is one of the most convincing
effects of what prayer can do, without either word
spoken or written.

A Christian lady, suffering and very infirm, conceived
a great affection for me, though we had never met ; and
she was often used in blessing to me, by lending my
poems widely among the sorrowful and weary, in the
extensive neighborhood in which she had a large circle
of friends. I longed to be helpful to her, but had no
clear way to do what I desired.

She suffered from great depression of spirits, and
could not enter into the joy of the Lord, or the full
enjoyment of his presence ; and this not from ignorance
of the glorious freedom the Lord accords his people,
not from a lack of knowledge of his sufficiency, but
from bodily infirmity of a peculiar nature. She waited
for her joy, when she should behold the King in his
beauty. We had never met. A long distance separated
us. I was shut out from all Christian intercourse and testimony, enjoying his gracious will, the joyful realization
of Him whom I had found as a " shadow of a great rock
in a weary land." One Sunday this lady was much on my
mind ; we were alike shut up to God. Suddenly I was led
to pray for her to share the joy that thrilled my being.
He had Himself opened to me the Scriptures. I could
not share with any the manna that fed me ; but I could
share the joy, and I asked for her to partake of it. For
many others my heart was drawn out, for counsel and
help and blessing ; but for none other could I ask this gift
of joyful praise. I felt richer for giving, and stronger
for working. But when the evening fell. the Enemy came
in like a flood. The joy in the Lord was of the Lord, but
I could no longer rejoice. My heart, overrunning with
praise, became full of doubt as to whether I had really
prayed *at all* for my poor sad friend. I became faithless and unbelieving ; and the morning that had broken
without clouds went down with a comprehension of what
spiritual depression really meant, for experimentally I
knew little of it.

The following evening brought me a letter dated from
the very hour my conflict and depression began. It

ran thus: "*Beloved Sister,*— Surely you have been praying for me this morning. I am relieved entirely of my pain and pressure, and my joy is so great that I have been singing hymns of praise all day in my bed. I could not contain my happiness." She had a remarkably sweet voice, and of wonderful power. Surely the strains must have reached some weary heart. We know that it was a glad offering to the God of Bethel. Satan had watched to destroy my strength; but the eye of Him who never slumbers nor sleeps, watched too. Oh, what a Lord we serve! Our covenant-keeping God is faithful who promised.

I needed nothing more to give me the certainty that *all* my prayers had been accepted. Thus the pitiful and tender Father sends his messengers with the oil and the wine to his fainting followers.

How weak is the foolish heart to listen to the voice of the enemy, instead of returning to the *written* Word, however little inclined, where some new view of the covenant of grace may be brought forth to meet each attack of Satan, if we persevere in the strength of the Conqueror!

In David's earliest combat he slew the giant, but later the son of one of the giants thought to slay him with a new sword; but not even a *new* sword could harm the man that God protected.

Perhaps this sudden shadow and depression taught me the blessed privilege of remembering my poor friend, and the joy that her brief note carried to me was the return of prayer into my own bosom.

"Whoso is wise and will observe these things, even

they shall understand the loving-kindness of the Lord,"
" and praise of one made joy for twain " But are we
too dull of hearing? Had she not shared her joy with
me, how great would have been my loss!

Some in extremity ask prayer from prayerful friends,
who share the burden but never partake of the praise
when the burden has been removed ; and thus the name
of the Lord is not magnified, nor the the souls that
shared the watch edified or refreshed.

One requests prayer for more of the Holy Sprit, yet
does not put himself in the position to receive it. He
is indulging in malice, unkindness, or worldliness.
There is often a kind of Popish superstition mingling
with requests for prayer ; as if the work in the soul
could be effected by a fellow-man, and he put not a finger
to the burden, while the responsibility is thrown off his
own shoulders, — not taking into account that God,
whose name is Love, is also a righteous God.

In regard to prayer for others and with others, we
need more preparation than we often ·give. When the
heart is moved by pity and sympathy, it seems to
enter on the service without waiting on the Lord ; and
nature's fruit, even of pity and sympathy, without the
Spirit, has no value within the veil. It is possible that
without this you may wound where He would heal, and
soothe when He is waking the soul to discipline. Those
who have passed this way comprehend in these hours of
lassitude and exhaustion how the soul shrinks from the
well-meant but distressing machinery so often used in
visitations of the sick.

He who knows what the heart needs, can alone give

the word, and enable you to console or strengthen,
sometimes in one way and sometimes in another. Re-
hoboam "did evil, because he prepared not his heart to
seek the Lord." (2 Chron. xii. 14.) And " Jotham
became mighty, *because* he prepared his ways before the
Lord." (2 Chron. xvii. 6.)

I was ill in a strange place, and many hearts were
moved with kindness toward me, and wished to minister to me. Among my visitors was a young pastor,
who seemed to understand my needs better than others.
He would pray for a few minutes, or tell me some news
of blessing, or repeat or read a few verses, and go
softly away, leaving me refreshed and thankful. When
I was better I inquired of him, " Where did you learn
such short prayers? Have you ever been very ill?"
" Yes, indeed," he replied with a smile ; " and it was in
my own sickness that I learned their value. Some of
my dear brethren visited me. They prayed for the
church, and the state, and the heathen, and foreign and
home missions, etc. ; and by the time they had arrived
at my case, I was generally fainting and could not hear
a word they said, or remember anything they had been
praying for " Few that I have known equalled him in
his ministry to the sick. His gentleness and quick
sympathy had been experimentally exercised by his
own need. " He that waiteth on his master shall be
honored" ; and he waited, and the Lord honored him
by using him and blessing him.

" Seeing then that we have a great High-Priest, that
is passed into the heavens, Jesus the Son of God, let us
hold fast our professions. For we have not an High-

Priest which cannot be touched with the feeling of our infirmities ; but was in all points tempted like as we are, yet without sin. Let us therefore come boldly unto the Throne of Grace, that we may obtain mercy, and find grace to help in time of need." (Heb. iv. 14-16.)

The most ordinary occasions of daily life are channels of communication with God. and offer a wide field for prayer. When His presence is obscured, or when we are not realizing where our wisdom and strength are laid up, daily cares often become more distressing than great sorrows. Even supposing that you do not receive any answer to your ejaculatory prayer according to your mind. yet if you have committed it to Him whose eye is on all his works, you will have received blessing, for his sympathy and love are with you. The very act of acknowledging Him will nourish the inner life, so quickly disturbed by the world's strife and snares.

Meanwhile there are seasons that demand sustained prayer, when we need special counsel and direction, when the accuser of the brethren stands by us to resist our approach to the Throne of Grace ; and when we rise from our knees, Satan tempts us to believe that we have nothing gained from our prayers and tears.

Let not the Evil One wrest from you your praise for prayer answered, nor seduce you to believe that you would have arrived at the same results if you had not prayed, or that it has only been granted to some one who has more fervently interceded than yourself ; for this puts the glory on man, and not on the finished work and intercession of Christ. Do not entertain this *doubt:* it

is an evil spirit who will quickly take to himself seven
other spirits more wicked than himself. If you have believed in the faithfulness of God, and appealed to Him
alone to grant the petition you laid before Him, then
believe that this faithful God has given it, and praise.
Have faith to believe that *your* prayers have wrought.
" The dead praise not the Lord!" " The living shall
praise thee, as I do this day." .

Such a season I recall when seeking the solution of
one of the deepest mysteries of my life, that affected
my own way, and my peace, and my understanding of
the Lord's will. I knew the unravelling of it must
come from Himself; I could only go to Him who
knoweth all things and can do all things, and like
Daniel, wait before Him.

Before I rose from my knees the hour struck that
called me elsewhere. I had gained no light on the
matter, but I had been enabled to cast my burden on
the Lord, and was content now to wait for what I asked,
until I entered into the kingdom of my Father. But
as I rose, I realized with a clearness most terrible the
taunt of the enemy, " What have you gained by your
long prayer for that which you can never secure?"

I confess I was startled, the suggestion swept over
my soul with such a withering. Satanic power; but I
remained still, and after a struggle I was able to say.
" I have received faith to wait until all mysteries shall
be revealed: I have left it all with Jesus." It seemed
to impart confidence and peace to my soul as I repeated
the words aloud. The Lord is oftentimes more honored by the faith that waits and trusts Him because

He is faithful, than even by the exulting praise that grasps the reply to our petition.

A few hours later there was placed in my hand a letter which fully answered my prayer, — as impossible for me to have expected as it was possible for God to give. The writer could not comprehend, neither was it given to any but myself to understand, what my prayer had wrought, or in what form He had replied to my wrestling supplication.

> "So out of all my griefs there grew
> The strength and joy to praise anew."

Souls knit in the bonds of heavenly love and sympathy may deepen our joys and lighten our sorrows, and by hearty counsel assist us to comprehend the way of the Lord, if they themselves have travelled the same path. But there are sorrows too deep for even a brother's hand to touch, and mysteries that only Daniel's God can solace; keep such for "Jesus only." It is worth the anguish to recognize the tender hand of Him who came to bind up the broken heart, and comfort them that mourn. Therefore "be strong, yea, be strong." We must learn to slay the lion in solitude, before we can stand in the face of two armies to meet the giant.

The temptation to relax closet prayer, and the conflict that so often awaits the believer, where he receives light for his way, and strength for his work, and peace for his soul, shows us that it is the place of power. Be not dismayed at the enemy that waits to trouble you. (Phil. i. 29, 30.) Is it a sense of sin that keeps you

afar off? It is the blood that maketh atonement, and
that blood is shed for you. You kneel to tell your sorrow and ask for help or deliverance from Him who can
alone counsel or comfort you; but your heart seems
swallowed up in the anguish still untold, and you think
no prayer has passed your lips, only the groan of unutterable woe: but have you not gone to the feet of the
Man of Sorrows acquainted with grief, and is not the
Holy Comforter unfolding the desires that your dumb
lips cannot utter, as you have asked faintly for grace
to meet temptations that assail you, and wandering
thoughts arise like a flock of birds, to be driven away
only for another return?

Wait, persevere, — the wandering thought can be
brought into subjection; but seek not to deal with the
wandering thought, for that will elude your vigilance;
but deal with Him who has led captivity captive, and
who will never let you seek his face in vain.

The heart, in defiance of all your effort, seems cold
and senseless and dull, as if grace had never renewed
it; as if the fresh springs had never fertilized it; as if
the Holy Spirit had never bathed it in his light, or
wakened it into gladness. Why is it so? Ah, why!
There is no promise that summer shall last all the year,
no covenant that the human shall be superhuman. We
dwell in a mysterious tabernacle, while waiting to be
clothed upon with our house from heaven. We are
compassed with infirmity, ignorant, and often out of
the way, impatient, and mistrustful of the only Hand
that can help us! Our help is in Him who is exalted
into all power in heaven and on earth, who is not one

who cannot be touched with the feeling of our infirmities.

Wait, believe in his love. Do not rise up and go away, as if He refused to listen to you. Tell Him your barrenness, your emptiness, your wanderings; you wish it otherwise, but you do not tell Him this. The will is there to spread your case before Him, but the way you know not. "Have faith in God."

Maybe long ago you prayed for grace, and you have not watched unto prayer. Now He lets you feel the need of that grace. Do not kneel down and expect at once effusions of heavenly joy to wither up the roots of sin, that henceforth you may know neither conflict nor sorrow. All the Shepherd's own must bear the Shepherd's mark, the mark of the "Man of Sorrows"; "but when He putteth forth his own sheep He goeth before them, and the sheep follow Him, for they know his voice."

Often He afflicts in answer to prayer, for a deeper knowledge of Himself, and to show forth some of those miracles of his power to establish the hearts of those that trust in Him, when He is about to bring them with a strong hand and powerful arm into the place of blessing, in the sight of *their* enemies and his. (Rom. ix. 17.)

The deep mysteries of faith are not given to the lukewarm and the idle, but to those who are "*watching* thereunto with all perseverance and supplication," and who make no bargain as to the way the Lord shall lead them. (Heb. ii. 10.)

Do not call on prayerful friends to seek for you

what you are too slothful patiently to labor for yourself. Watch and wait and pray, not one morning or
one evening, when your heart is tender, but when no
conscious joy makes the act of prayer a pleasant service.

What is called " faith" must be tried in the furnace,
purified and prepared for the Master's use. If it
endureth, then only is it "precious faith."

When the tide recedes, the shore glitters in the sunshine ; to a casual glance a child might say gems were
scattered there. They are but valueless pebbles and
broken glass, that will wound unwary feet ; so is much
of the empty profession of the present day, — it has no
value but to attract the senses by externals, and to win
the eye of the world, not the heart of God. (1 Cor.
ii. 5.)

It is not for us to know what amount of faith is
needed for the return of blessing. We are told to pray
and not faint, and that the touch of the Holy One can
save. (Mark v. 28-34.) As long as we are in this
body so wonderfully constituted, we only feel at intervals the transcendent joy that awaits us when we shall
be " changed." (1 Cor. ii. 8, 9.) But the infirmities
and sufferings and thorns in the flesh are but Marahs
and Meribahs to show forth the love and power of Him
who has called us to consider his ways.

God's way, answered and unanswered prayer, often
remains in mystery, but we must believe that there is
a higher motive than the mere acquiescence in a
request. We can only give light thereon, and uphold
our often sinking heart by remembering that we have

given ourselves into the hands of Him, who seeth not as man seeth, and who when on earth, judged not after the sight of his eyes, neither reproved after the hearing of his ears.

It has been productive of increased confidence in the Lord to prove, when He has graciously allowed me, the effect of answered or unanswered prayer on individual souls ; not looking on our own things only, but also on the things of others.

A friend of mine visited me one evening when I was worn out with prolonged sleeplessness. He was moved at the sight of my suffering, and as he rose to depart, compassionately asked me if I could suggest anything in which he could help me. I promptly replied, " Pray for me that the Lord will grant me sleep to-night." He seemed glad of the commission, and left, promising to see me in the morning on his way to the city.

A night of unbroken sleeplessness left me yet more exhausted, and I turned wearily from my desk, where letters awaiting replies had accumulated from day to day.

My friend called to inquire for me, and found me worse than the preceding day. I inquired, " Did you pray for me to sleep? I have not closed my eyes all night ! " He was confused, and frankly confessed that it had entirely escaped his memory, and then took his leave.

About ten minutes later I roused myself to arrange my papers, read my letters, and look over the work that lay before me. Suddenly my eyelids drooped, I fell back in a deep slumber, from which I awoke strengthened and refreshed, and not a little amazed at the peculiar manner in which it had seized me.

My visitor returned in the evening, and I hastened to tell him how graciously the Lord had accorded me sleep, though he had forgotten to ask it for me. His face lighted up with joy as he told me that he had left me with feelings of self-condemnation that he had so easily forgotten my suffering, and the only request I had made him. As he walked along he confessed it to the Lord, and prayed Him to give me sleep The Lord only waited for the confession and the supplication, and answered! Thus we trace the hand of a Father in giving or withholding, as seems good to Him for his wilderness family, whom He is preparing for their heavenly inheritancce.

But these answers are not always made evident; we walk by faith, not by sight, and we must believe that He has given us that which is good in his sight, so we can say, "Thy testimonies have I taken as a heritage forever; for they are the rejoicing of my heart." (Ps. cxix. 111.)

I know one who reaps openly what she sows in secret; and whether it be a national judgment or a stranger's salvation, oftentimes in the silence of her spirit the consciousness of the request granted has been changed to thanksgiving. When the Abyssinian captives called for England's help and prayer, she labored for their deliverance in faith and patient prayer, and the time of their release was evident to her by prayer being changed to thanksgiving before the telegram announced the fact to the country. "And many such things are with Him."

Often have I had to mourn over my persistent desire for friends and service, instead of being satisfied with the dealings of the Lord which shut me out of all outward testimony, and prepared me for the better service of waiting on Himself.

We are not to make work for ourselves, or to create ourselves providences, or much that is done will have to be undone, and much that mere human benevolence has led us to do will leave us to regret that we walked in sparks of our own kindling.

I made the acquaintance of one who appeared a spiritual Christian, who seemed to know the blessing of walking with God; and I thought she would teach me more of the things of God, of his ways and his grace and his dealings. I did not wait to prove if the Lord would have me leave the seclusion in which He had manifestly placed me for the work to which He had called me. I was thirsting for companionship in a dry and thirsty land, where there was no water. Instead of turning to the fountain of Israel, as often before, to renew my strength, waiting to know his will, I turned to empty cisterns.

Soon my self-chosen acquaintance avoided conversing with me, I knew not why. Her little knowledge of the things of eternity seemed exhausted, and a worldly guest arriving at the house, she shunned me altogether. One morning I found the two ladies engaged in cards, and the next day the same. My former companion remarked to me that I always left the room when they began their game. This brought us to the subject; and she replied, on my expressing surprise at her wasted time, that she consulted the Lord, not me.

" And did you really consult Him about *écarte?*" I inquired. " Yes," she answered readily, " and there is no harm if you do not play for money." It was in vain I set before her her own loss, and the evil example to the young people around her. I pondered if it were possibly from her ignorance : and remembering how often the Lord has to remind me of my foolishness and ignorance, I would not give her up.

I confess that only when my arguments failed, I began to feel the importance of the step I had taken in my own strength. But Jehoshaphat, when out of the way, cried to the Lord, and the Lord heard him ; so I cried to the Lord, and He heard me, and often since then I have felt i' the simplest wisdom to be silent after the testimony, which must be given, and use no human influence but to speak to God only until called by Him to action.

We are slow learners of the deep mysteries hid in the wisdom of God and the power of God. I asked the Lord whenever the lady touched the cards that she might be miserable until she had seen his will in the matter.

I lived principally in my own room, but only in the expression of wretchedness on her countenance when we met at the dinner-table did I learn that the Lord was dealing with her, and she confessed herself so miserable that she desired to leave the place. Nevertheless, she was prevented from so doing. Covert sneers and mockery met me on every side, so that I was more alone than ever, and now under different circumstances from what it appeared to me the Lord had chosen for me. As I passed the terrace overlooking the wide expanse of hill and valley in the first freshness of the morning, there still sat the unwearied card-players. But the matter was now not one that I *could* cast away by my own will, but it *was laid* on me to carry what I had perhaps unadvisedly taken up. . I prayed for the deliverance of one who seemed led captive by Satan at his will. Shortly the companion fell and injured her arm so that she could not hold the cards. and I could read in other things that the Lord was dealing. " But I kept all these things in my heart, neither told I any man." " The secret of the Lord is with them that fear Him," and many a service and to serve. Our enemies are his enemies ; the conflict is many a lesson are intended only for the soul that is called not visible to the sight of man, waged between the powers of darkness and Satan's conqueror. We do not now see the hand wither at the word (1 Kings xiii. 4), neither do we see the disobedient servant slain by a lion in the way : nevertheless God is not mocked, man eats the fruit of his doing in some manner, the grace saves, and the blood cleanseth. All things may seem against us, but all things are working together for good to them that love God, and that " good " is everlasting. Hereafter we shall read the answer to many a cry we thought unheard and unheeded, and behold the hand of the Lord was even here stretched out against our adversaries, and accomplished the real defeat to those who seemed to *us* to triumph. We have to do with Eternal Realities, a " very present God," a great " I AM," who uses even

the weakness and foolishness of his children for purposes of ultimate blessing. Eternity only will disclose
the answers to many a smothered groan and tear, wrung
forth by cruelty which here receives no punishment.
Something of this we may perceive even now, and
learn from it much more we might know if we walked
closely with Him. But oh, how much more we shall
know hereafter! The Philistines may come down upon
you and distress you, but if your arm has been in the
strength of the mighty God of Jacob, you have not
failed though all seemed against you. How often have
I pleaded his promise on the day of affliction and
oppression! and never did it fail me. (Ex. xxii.)

A week passed of great outward discomfort; the
visitor recovered the use of her wounded hand, and
with the renewed games arose renewed hostility to me.
How gladly would I have departed! but I feared to do
so without some intimation of the Lord's will, lest I
should fly from the cross; but as He was sensibly near
me when alone, I remained, waiting *his* time.

Henceforth I was dumb, and shut up from testimony.
I could no longer say, " I kept silence save from good
words, but it was *pain and grief to me.*" But I was
dumb because He did it, dumb from the power of the
Lord on me. At some remark I made the poor card-
player joined the boisterous laughter that followed, which
led me to inquire why so simple an observation had called
it forth. Though I had not addressed myself to her,
she replied that she would laugh where and when she
liked and as much as she liked, without my permission.
My nerves unstrung and my heart heavy with the antag-

onistic influences around, I cried to the Lord in the solitude of my chamber, "If I am thy servant and have
spoken at thy word, show me thine hand in this matter";
and after a while I was able to lean my weary heart on
Him who is the helper of the helpless. A deep peace
fell on me, and I was at rest.

The silence of the sweet summer evening was broken
by bursts of loud laughter and merriment coming from
the pair who occupied an adjoining room. The night
came, and the laugh continued; the morning broke and
it ceased not, and that terrible laughter echoed in
awful peals through the otherwise silent corridor.
Others saw in it only an extraordinary fit of prolonged
hysteria. I saw in it the finger of God. (1 Chron. v.
20.)

I have reason to believe that if we keep our watch
from our watch-tower, in patient expectation, we shall
constantly see that the Lord is not unmindful of our
desire for His glory. I have often found it so before
any special trial of faith : we know his faithfulness, —
how often do we mistrust it! — but He remembers we
are dust.

Requests are sometimes answered in the *exact* form
of our prayer offered, and this I have remarked where
the temptation has been that I have *not prayed* at all.
Requests are sometimes given in the usual form of
prayer offered. While travelling in the East, a worldly
young man, who seemed to have no real interest in heavenly things, desired to introduce to me a new acquaintance who, in spite of his Christianity, greatly attracted
him. With such an introduction I was not prepared to

find a fellow-pilgrim on his way to the home of the many mansions ; he inspired me with deep interest. I could not realize that one in whom vitality seemed so strong could be in a position to require the climate so seldom sought until all else fails.

Not many were our interviews, but we were drawn together by that one bond which makes strangers in a strange land brethren in the same hope, the same inheritance, the same fatherland.

Some time passed, and I missed his accustomed visits. One day when the Campsee wind was blowing a hurricane, blinding us with the fine, penetrating dust even in the carefully closed chambers. I was startled by the entrance of my new friend, who had arrived from another part of the city, to visit me. I could not but gently reprove him for his temerity in venturing out on such a day. With a sad smile he answered me, " The hurricane cannot harm me so much as those I have left to come to you ; let me stay with you." I consented, thankful to be used in any way in that desert land, to one laid down in the prime of his youth. when he longed to serve the Lord he loved We spoke long and uninterruptedly together ; but after that day I remarked a sensible change in his appearance. symptoms that I had been accustomed to trace in those I had watched sinking under the progress of the same insidious disease. Then I felt for the first time that he was sealed for death. When we could not meet, I sometimes sent him a few lines, a text, or book, so that he might feel that he was unforgotten. and not be oppressed by the sense of isolation which often presses

so heavily on those sick and dying in a foreign land.
Often when he left me I asked who would close those
frank eyes, that now, still radiant in hope, met my own
so gratefully; and who would watch over him to the
last. I knew the Saviour who loved him would be
there; but the hearts of loving ones still in the body
quail at the thought of strangers gathering the last
farewell. the last sigh, and my thought often wandered
on to the widowed mother who was watching for him,
and could not forego the hope of his restoration. I
prayed that life, waning so fast. might yet be granted
to him to reach his native land, his mother's arms, and
leave them only for our Father's home on high.

We parted, conscious that it was our last meeting on
earth. He went up the country. and I heard of him no
more. Still my prayer followed him. that he might
return to England and be spared to die in his mother's
arms. I did not even know his place of abode, and he
was now beyond the reach of any communication.
Often I heard of such miracles of healing from a winter and spring in the East, that the suggestion would
sometimes arise, Would it be possible for him to be
raised again to health? But it always ended in prayer
that he might reach his English home and the mother
who watched for him. How often I longed to know if
my prayer was granted! and as often I said, "It is
impossible that I can ever learn it until we meet in the
presence of the King."

Two years or more after this, a dear friend of mine
heard of a lady ill at a hotel; and with the ever-lov-
ing care for the stranger, and bent on service for the

Master, she went to offer her sympathy and Christian
service. It was the widowed mother of the young traveller, the subject of so many of my thoughts and prayers. In relating some particulars of her sickness, and
her sorrows, she dwelt on the mercy which had guided
and guarded her beloved son to England. At the last
he was too weak for the proposed journey to their
home. She met him at the port, and she had the sweet
mercy of sharing his last days on earth. Then he placed
in her hands the little memorials of our brief friendship
as a legacy of love to her, and passed away in joyous
anticipation of his Lord's welcome home, *and died in
his mother's arms*. It was my privilege to give her the
few details of our meeting, and she joined me in praising the Lord for his faithfulness and his love ; and we
could both say, '' His compassions fail not ; they are
new every morning.'' (Lam. iii. 23.)

Ah ! why do we stand so far off in our prayers for
ourselves and others ? Why cannot we confide in Him
implicitly, and trust Him to bring to pass all that shall
be for his glory and the well-being of those so precious
to Him ? (Jer. xxxi. 3.)

'' Watch unto prayer.'' The little cloud out of the
sea, like a man's hand, will come at last, for under the
wings of the cherubim are the hands of a man.
Watch and be not weary ; though it be the sixth time,
yet go the seventh time. Watch ! for if God has
promised it will surely come, it will not tarry. '' Wait
thou only upon God,'' for the Lord is good to them
that wait for him, and to the soul that seeketh Him.
There is sometimes more difficulty in trusting the Lord

for the occurrences of every-day life than in what appears to us a more important necessity : but I have specially remarked that in those matters which had no *individual* interest or need, but only embraced the well-being of others and the glory of God, such prayers have been marked by some peculiar feature of individuality in which we could never be mistaken.

I became acquainted with a lady and her family recently converted ; her son had left her to join his regiment, then in the expectation of an engagement. Her joy on his conversion was saddened by the thought that his life might not be spared to testify for the Lord, who had dealt wondrously with him. One morning I joined her in special prayer for him, that even now, or on the battle-field, that testimony might still be given. As I read the letter which conveyed the news to his mother of his critical position, I could scarcely realize that this soul, so full of simple faith and understanding of the ways of God, had only turned from darkness to light in the short space of a few weeks. That morning there was much to say to the Lord in behalf of the absent son : we prayed for the regiment, for the sick and the wounded and the dying ; we petitioned for his life to be spared, but whether he lived or died, that he might leave a testimony for others of the blessed change that the power of the Holy Spirit had wrought in him. We had reached this clause in our request when we were interrupted ; never again was our prayer renewed, and never again have we met.

Towards the close of the summer, while in one of the crowded watering-places in England, I met a lady with

an invalid brother, little prepared for the future which
seemed to await him. He had just returned to England, invalided, with some of his regiment. I cannot
tell why I felt so great a desire to see him, for his
sister did not by any means encourage me to do so;
nevertheless, I could not give up the hope that the Lord
would make the way if he had any service for me. I
had been warned that he would not have any pleasure
in receiving my visit, and advised to give up my proj-
ect; but such an oppression and uneasiness disturbed
me when I did so, that after prayer I determined to go
without any preparation of the invalid. It was in vain
I was told that I must not be surprised, when I walked
in at one door, if he should walk out at the other!
This was not very encouraging, and I had nothing to sustain me but the hope it was of the Lord, and in making
the trial, and judging by results if I were walking according to the will of the Lord, or after the imagination of
my own heart. I went. The sister received me alone,
and gave me no hope of an introduction to her brother;
but as she mentioned the detachment to which he
belonged, the door opened, and the invalid entered the
room. So far from quitting it when he saw me, he
advanced towards me with a frank and courteous greeting, and we were friends at once.

· His sister leaving the room, we were alone. I dared
not stand on ceremony; and after asking some details
of his health, — and indeed he seemed fast sinking into
the grave, — I entered on the subject nearest my heart.
My thankful joy at the way the Lord had led me made
the fire in my own soul burn in ardent desire for the

salvation of another. I know not now what I said. I
can but remember that I pleaded for Jesus. My lis-
tener manifested much emotion, and remained silent
until I paused ; and then slowly, as if recalling the past,
he said, " How strange that you should speak thus ! I
could almost believe it was a brother officer, who spoke
to me the night before we were ordered out. He came
to my tent at night, and sitting down by my bed (for
I was ill), he said to me, ' To-morrow we may die. Are
you prepared for *that?* Are you saved? I am.' ' *No,*'
I replied, ' I am *not* saved.' He spoke as you have
spoken, and prayed with me as you have done, and I believed I was saved ; but since then I cannot think that
any heart can have secured the grace of God, and have
the wicked thoughts that come into *my* heart." As he
bent down his pale face on his hands, there was evidence of great mental suffering, as well as physical.
The washing of water by the Word, and the precious
Blood that cleanseth, seemed what he needed. The
utter depravity of the old nature, and the war of the
spirit with the flesh, seemed a new light to him.

It was an hour of deepest interest to me ; but what
joy filled my soul when, in answer to the question as to
the name of the brother officer who had paid him the
midnight visit, he gave me that of the beloved absent
son for whom we had entreated testimony. Then I heard
that the Hand which had led me just where I was, had
covered his head in the day of battle and given him
testimony on the battle-field ; thus teaching me that
whether we know or whether we know not the sweet
odor of the meat-offering, Emmanuel's perfect and

accepted merits had carried up the brief and interrupted prayer, and called me to adore once again the
wondrous ways by which the faithfulness of God is
proved. Oh, what has such gracious unveiling of his
ways revealed to me! More of the heart of God!
How often have I repeated this: " That I have prayed
for, I shall never read until I have passed out of this
land of shadows." O, ye of little faith, wherefore didst
thou doubt! If one regret could sadden the glory
which God has prepared for them that love Him, it
would be that we mistrusted the love of Him whose
every thought to us was one " of peace, and not of
evil "; who delighteth in mercy, and loves with an everlasting love. But how often can it be said of us, " But
though He had done so many miracles among them, yet
they believed not on Him." (John xii. 7.)

In many cases the answers to our prayers are not
revealed to us; but nothing is impossible to Him who
holds creation in his hand, and whose resources are
infinite in discovering or concealing the results of our
prayers. How many heavenly surprises await us in
our Father's house, when we shall at last confess that
every prayer, however broken and feeble and imper-
fect to our own view, however impossible to others
even to expect or hope for, however mean in the sight
of the wise of this world, are all gathered and received
in the censer of our Great High-Priest, — " accepted in
the Beloved," and were all (seen or unseen) considered by Him, and eventually working to the glory of
Him who has bidden us " Pray and not faint."

Signs are still visible to those who walk with God

according to his word, and not after the imagination of their own hearts. If we have committed our way to the Lord, desiring not our own will but his will, not our pleasure but his pleasure, we may confidently rely that the most timid believer, if he watch, shall read that will aright. I have numberless examples of this, and in some cases had I imagined the will of the Lord opposed to me in the first obstacle, I should have mistaken it; but by waiting and praying and watching, I have found that it was the way I should go.

Much of failure arises from lack of knowing if we are doing our own will, and the impatience to go forward *before* the Lord. rather than following Him. He has said, " I will guide thee with mine eye," and the eyes of all that wait on Him in patient prayer shall be enlightened; those who trust Him shall not be confounded.

We need definite requests in our prayers. Oftentimes our circumstances of daily necessity are those in which He replies to our petition for growth in grace. We find that the present help includes the answer to some prayer of long standing. We are prone to expect to handle spiritual gifts as we do some tangible result of our prayers. God is not unmindful of his covenant: grace shall be given; nay, grace has been given if we could believe it *is* ours. Blessing *must* follow persevering prayer. " He is not unrighteous to forget your works and labors of love, which ye have showed towards his name." Only seek his face continually, and though there is no promise of natural satisfaction in our prayer, yet persevere. He has said, He is nigh to them that call upon him.

There is no greater proof of the influence of prayer with God than his withholding the power of carrying the request we desire, if not according to his will ; as Samuel mourned for Saul, but he could no longer pray for him. This is the contrast to Rom. viii. 26. " He that searcheth the hearts knoweth what is the mind of the Spirit, because He maketh intercession for the saints according to the will of God." Perhaps those weak in faith are allowed to see more results than others ; as the spiritual senses are exercised, we learn to seek more intimately the Lord's will and the Lord's glory. We are content to leave times and seasons in the Father's hand. It is the *heart* prayer He waits for.

A friend (one who stands before the Lord) told me that late one night he was called by a confirmed infidel to visit his dying son. The young man imbibed the same principles and lived the same life of sin. He entered the chamber, where a single candle on the man- tel·piece shed its light on the face of the stranger. Death had begun his work, — the death that dies not. The servant of God set before him the hope even for the eleventh hour : the love of the Father, the blood of the Crucified, the power of Him who came to die for the sins of the world. All in vain ! No answer could he obtain ; not a word passed the lips of the dying man, whose fast-glazing eyes stared wildly into his own. He threw himself on his knees by the departing soul, and strove to pray, — strove, but in vain. No access was given his faith ; and hope, which had so often sus- tained him in carrying the message of mercy to sinners, seemed bound up in his breast, and the prayer rebounded back. His tongue clove to his mouth; he closed his eyes, and cast himself on the power of the Mighty to save. Then there came distinct and clear the voice of the Holy Spirit that thrilled his being : " Pray not thou for this people, neither lift up cry nor prayer for them, neither make intercession to Me, for I will not hear thee." A groan echoed through that death chamber; the candle that lighted the face of the dying infidel sank in the socket, and was extinguished. The servant of God opened his eyes. All was darkness and silence and death ; and feeling for his hat, he rushed out of the house, and looking up to the calm, starlit sky, he thanked the God of all grace that he was not an infidel.

The sound of singing came on his ear. He crossed the street, and was led into an upper room, — a startling contrast to the solemn scene he had just left. Supported in the arms of a loving Christian woman lay a dying girl, her name once proverbial for outward sin. Her face beamed like the face of an angel. The joy of that departing soul was beyond all expression, and the power of Christ's love was felt by every one in that death chamber, that to all assembled there was the very portal of heaven. She witnessed that Jesus was the joy of her heart, and that she was dying in his powerful arms ; and with a joyful voice joined in singing with the brethren around her her last song on earth : —

> " One there is above all others,
>   Oh, how He loves ! "

And with this her spirit departed. Those who had felt the power and presence of Christ in the chamber of this

converted soul, rescued from Satan and sin, and translated into the kingdom of God's dear Son, passed the
hours until morning in a neighboring dwelling, singing
and weeping for joy, praying and praising

" Look not to the clouds ; for he that observeth the
wind shall not sow, and he that regardeth the clouds
shall not reap. . . . Make the valley full of ditches,
for they shall be full of water." (2 Kings iii.) Not
from the accustomed resources of nature, perhaps, to
which you have formerly sought and used aforetimes,
but in new and unexpected manner He will surely give
you the living water for which you wait.

He could give his own gifts direct from Himself without our intervention, but He chooses to make use of his
children's hands to dig the channels to bring blessing to
others and glory to his name. Do all you can for the
souls you seek, testify of what the Lord is to you, what
He will be to them ; give the book, the tract, write the
letter, offer the courtesy which may attract, and expect
a blessing, — but the Lord alone can give it. You cannot reach the haughty sinner, the giddy worldling, the
vain scorner, until the sweet savor of the sinless offering, the merits of a perfect Saviour, perfume your
prayers. Then shall living water flow into the channels your weak hands have made. " He that believeth
on me," as the Scripture hath said, " out of his belly
shall flow rivers of living water." (John vii. 38.)

Spiritual life must be nourished, and if we " covet
the best gifts " we must be prepared to receive them.
Do you long for a full measure of the Spirit, an understanding heart, answers to your prayers? It is well

to remember, Am I prepared for the blessing? Be no: negligent, for "by much slothfulness the building decayeth, and through idleness of the hands the house droppeth through." (Ex. xi. 18.) Make channels for the waters of life. Prepare the way before the Lord. Be instant in prayer. Be faithful in watching. Seek Him, but "make the valley full of ditches," and He will not withhold from you the living waters. (2 Kings iii.) Did you once make them, and are they now choked with clay and strange vanities? Then "wheel out the rubbish," that there be no impediment for the stream of blessing to your own heart. And how shall you stand in the desolate valley of dry bones? The Chief Shepherd has said, "Behold I, even I will both search my sheep and seek them out." Will He not use *your* hand and give them drink out of your channels, if you have made them ready, and give drink to his thirsty ones and refreshment to his weary ones? And are they prepared, and as yet you see no water?

CHAPTER III.

" OUR sister did not write books, but she left her footsteps to teach us the way she went to God." Thus spoke an Indian chief over the dead body of a missionary's wife, ere the earth enclosed it. She had led him to believe in the truth of God, and the wisdom of God, and the love of God. The untaught chief had *considered* her. At the return of every Sabbath, he came down from his mountain home uninvited and joined in the midday meal of the teacher, won by the living power of Christianity in the words and life of his gen‧ tle hostess. He took knowledge of her that she had been with Jesus.

Oh, better than the printed book is the living epistle known and read of all men, a record of the grace of God in everlasting remembrance !

When I have pondered on the precious life given to Christ the Lord, and laid down for Him in South Africa, I have been led to remember how many hidden witnesses (Is. xliii. 12) the Lord watches over, whose doings are not written on the printed page, where the praise and blame of men can sully them, whose only record is in the hearts that have been blessed through their instrumentality, but whose names are known to Him (Ex. xxxiii. 12 ; Is. xlv. 3), and written in the Lamb's Book of Life. Such will be among the illustrious witnesses in the kingdom that is not of this world ; and already the Lord has said unto them, " I know thy works, and thy labors, and thy patience " (Rev. ii. 2), though *here* unchronicled.

The body is one and hath many members, and all the members of that one body, being many, are one body. (1 Cor. xii.) One section of the church of Christ (the hidden ones of God) form the heart and lungs of the active members ; yet are they seldom recognized by the visible workers, who deem them cut off from service, *because* shut in with God. And those whose faith and patience and prayer flood the land for the sower, and strengthen the hand of the reaper, are scarcely owned or valued, save by Him who in the shadow of the rock is carrying out his appointed means for perfecting in light and glory his diadem of beauty. (Is. lxii. 3.)

Years of suffering and exhausted nerves, or secret household sorrows with which no human heart has sympathized, have left the soul of such with only the sacrifice of faith. " I *know* Whom I have believed," yet these hidden springs are sending forth in unconscious power streams of living water, and fertilizing barren lands. " Behold, we count them happy which endure ; ye have heard of the patience of Job, and have seen the end of the Lord, that the Lord is very pitiful and of tender mercy."

When the earth vibrated to the resurrection of her
Maker, and many saints that slept arose, the first-fruits
of Him who came to seek and to save, maybe some of
the hidden church were there. The names of those who
entered the heavenly gate opened to the King of glory
are unrecorded in Scripture, but known to Him who
calleth his sheep by their name, chosen of God and
precious. Doubtless in that heavenly train there were
members of his body, unrecognized by the scornful
multitude, and lightly esteemed by the disciples. It is
good to remember that He cutteth out the rivulets
among the rocks, and the springs run into the valleys,
and his eye seeth every precious thing. Not uncounted
are the sighs and groans of his prisoners ; not unseen
the tears that rise unbidden, hidden from all but Him.
The Master whose hand knows how to tune the harp of
a thousand strings, varies the trials and modulates the
praise by thus awaking the minor keys to contribute to
the perfected harmony of heaven.

As there are glades in the dark forests afar off that
the most enterprising traveller has never explored, and
valleys among the distant mountains the foot of man
has never trodden, and glorious created wonders above
the earth and beneath the waters no eye has ever gazed
on, no hand has ever measured ; so there are peculiar
treasures concealed beneath the shadow of the Rock,
only to be revealed when the diadem is lifted up.
Many an one, like Joash, is hidden in the house of God
six years in safety, until the set time is fully come for
him to fill the position appointed him (2 Chron. xxii.
10-12), whether that position be in the sight of man

or in the eternal kingdom, to be recognized hereafter.
There is a hidden birth and a hidden life with which
man has nothing to do. "That which is born of the
flesh is flesh, and that which is born of the spirit is
spirit" (John iii. 6), and the mystery of this wondrous
transformation is often in the end solved to our sight.
The Lord has dealt with his servant alone; He has
taken him aside (Mark vii. 33); He has sighed over
his deaf stammerer, and at his word the string of his
tongue is loosed, and the multitude marvel. Ah, it is
no marvel that a man should hear and see and speak
when he has been alone with Jesus. Yea, he hears and
sees what the multitude know not, the results of which
alone are visible. When the blind man feels the touch
of the Divine Hand that has led him away from his fel-
lows, he sees who has done it all, and recognizes the
alpha and omega of divine life, — JESUS.

Who that knows Him, and the power of his resurrection, has ever regretted the fellowship of his sufferings
by which the knowledge of *Himself* was attained, and
the patient acceptance of which has maintained the
nearness to a crucified and risen Lord? For in conflict
and persecution and tribulation alone we learn the
fidelity of Him who has written and proved, "Fall
upon Me, and I will answer thee, and show thee great
and marvellous things that thou knowest not."

The heart-breaking of God's people is but the wine-
press, the crushing of the grape for the new wine, for
the kingdom rejoiceth the heart of God and man, and
wakens vintage songs of praise to the Great Husbandman. Nothing is lost; the refuse and vile only is cast

out. The affliction of those who desire not the knowledge of his name is but the crushing of poison berries,
and gives forth that which is evil, the fruit after its
own kind. It cannot afford nourishment or refreshment: men gather not grapes from thorns, and figs
of thistles; therefore, the end of them is rebellion and
curses, and " They shall be as dung upon the face of
the earth, for death is chosen rather than life." (Jer.
viii. 2, 3.)

You have asked the Lord to give you a fuller enjoyment and understanding of *Himself;* then be not surprised that He dries up the cistern, as a huge sweep of
a rising billow licks up the pools of standing water in
which our fair ocean flowers have flourished as in a
garden. You have prayed for a renewed hunger for
his word, and He silences the lips that once made music
in your heart, and the word of Him who smites is your
only refuge. And though you may not praise Him
while the blinding brine dims your eyes, yet the Lord
waiteth to be *gracious.* Be not faithless but believing.
" Blessed are all they that wait for Him." (Is. xxx.
12.)

Among my vineyard lessons, I watched a vine-
dresser ruthlessly cutting down the branches of the
trees that had hitherto sheltered the green grapes. The
time had arrived when there must be nothing between
the burning sun and the unripe fruit. The shadowing
boughs that had overhung them, and their own luxuriant leaves, must fall beneath the master's knife. They
were no longer needed, — they were impoverishing the
fruit that would form the vine! Among the fruitful

branches was a wild vine, throwing its graceful tendrils round the trellis, so that the fruit-bearing branches of the true vine might easily be mistaken for its own fruition. Many looking on it said, "How beautiful!" but the vine dresser could discern the true from the false, and said, "Why cumbereth it the ground?" and as its long flexile branches were untwined from the true vine, we saw that it had gained its position by clasping a peach-tree for its support, and its fine promise of fruit had fallen withered to the ground. So it is and will be with professors. I have remarked that it is the aged men who prune the choice vines. I have never seen but the hoary head engaged in this branch of the service.

Who that has brought forth fruit does not remember the hand that pruned what seemed to us our fairest branches of promise, and the sheltering bough in which we rejoiced (John xv. 2); and while we were denuded of all outward comeliness to the eyes of others, we were being prepared to bring forth fruit unto God.

You must be in a position of blessing to be blessed. If you desire to know more of Him you serve, you must meditate on his word and his dealings, and watch for Him in your daily life, counting nothing too mean to dispense with his blessing, and He will be found of you. He lays his hand upon the earthly, that we may recognize our only rest in the heavenly. When the pleasant places of the wilderness are dried up, then, only then, we betake ourselves to the God of Bethel! Trials do not always lead the soul to trust in the love of God, if the heart is only occupied with

the circumstance, rather than with Him who is mould-
ing it for our chastening and instruction. Every step
nearer to the Lord is in deeper fellowship with the
Man of Sorrows, and therefore more dependent on
his sympathy, and his sympathy alone. You must
learn something more of cross-carrying, before you
know the power of the Lord to enable you to carry it
to his glory. Hezekiah eagerly accepted healing;
nevertheless, he soon forgot the gracious dealing of the
Lord, because he was more intent upon the healing
than the Great Healer, and thought more of displaying
what man could handle and admire, rather than setting
forth the power and love of God, less tangible to the
natural heart. The Lord had worked great deliverances
for Asa, but in his sickness he sought not to the Lord,
but to the physicians only, thus making flesh his arm.
"Every branch that beareth not fruit, He taketh
away, and every branch that beareth fruit, He purgeth
it, that it may bring forth more fruit." Service and
testimony lie ever around the child of God in his
daily life ; he may be hidden from man, but God has
said, "Walk before Me." You may be surrounded by
those with whom you have no sympathy, who misap-
prehend and misrepresent you ; but God alone reads
the heart or knows what seed of patience and faith and
hope from your own life may find rest in theirs, though
to you the soil seems all barren ; but it may be ordained
for you to scatter the imperceptible seed to be found
after many days. He has said, "I will be a wall of
fire round about her"; and the wall against which we
are frequently spending our strength to break down is

the one that hedges up the way of the wilful child, and burns up the pleasant things he delights in, so that he cannot find the paths he thinks more suitable for the attainment of that which he desires.

The discontent that sometimes fills the heart laid by from active service seldom arises until it has lost some opportunity of blessing, or some occasion of testimony has passed by unimproved. Then he looks away with longing desire for a work exactly suited to his hand, something for which he has a natural aptitude, a work he cannot do now, — why? Because the door is closed, the bolt is drawn, and the prisoner of the Lord is laid aside to suffer *his* will, rather than enjoy his own. We are a spectacle to angels and principalities and powers in heavenly places, who learn from us the might of the glorious sacrifice of the Lamb of God, and his manifold mercies and wisdom to a worm of the dust, called, chosen, and sanctified by his own will and power. Let Him do what he will with his own, his way is past finding out. His way is in the sea, and his path in the great waters, and his footsteps are not seen.

We are prone to expect some conscious power in service and testimony, yet at the same time asserting, and in *measure* believing, that we walk by faith, not by sight. Gideon was poor, and the least in his father's house. He was a timid man, and needed a sign for every step in following the Lord ; and became mighty with the few men appointed him, when with a larger army he would have failed. " Not many wise men after the flesh, not many mighty, not many noble are called : but God hath chosen the foolish things of the world to confound the wise ; and God hath chosen the weak things of the world to confound the things which are mighty ; and base things of the world, and things which are despised, hath God chosen, yea, and things which are not, to bring to naught things that are : that no flesh should glory in his presence." (1 Cor. i. 26– 29.) Oh, that this lesson were constantly conned by the church of Christ, which is certainly not com-posed of the noble and mighty and wise ! Then we should see the followers of the Lamb, meek and " strong in the Lord, and the power of his might," not desiring that which the Lord has not commanded, nor discouraged because they have to watch and not weary, and pray and not faint. Such as stand by night in the house of the Lord never serve alone. Though unseen of man, they are taught and blessed of God. A special service belongs to the secluded priest ; the Levites had no light service in the sanctuary, but the sweetest of all services was accorded them, — " to stand every morn-ing to thank and praise the Lord, and likewise at even." (1 Chron. xxiii. 30.) Blessed are those hidden thus in the clefts of the Rock, unseen of man, but precious in his sight. He will fashion them and use them if they are faithful to his word and his teaching. Such need a constant reliance on Him who has placed them in a position none would have chosen for himself ; one more dependent, more humiliating, more open to temptation of discouragement, depression, and discontent than any other, but yet necessarily cast on his tender care in the least matter, who has the unfailing resource of the wisdom and strength of Him who " has his treasures in earthen vessels, that the excellency of the power may be of God, and not of us." (2 Cor. iv. 7.)

One day in the heat of an Italian summer, I left the house for the shadow of the cypress-trees that flanked a large garden that surrounded the villa where I resided. The air was heavy with the scent of flowers, and the bloom and fruit of the lemon-trees. Distressed by the heat and cast down by my lack of power, mental and physical. I sat down wearily by the fountain, whose falling waters made the only sounds that broke the stillness of the burning afternoon. Around the marble basin the plants and flowers in their stone vases were drooping or dead. yet the water was so near that their fading leaves were reflected back. though broken by the troubled mirror ; but not a drop of the crystal shower refreshed them.

As the lines of water rose and fell monotonously in two straight lines, not one drop on the fading life around it, it seemed to me an illustration of a selfish Christian, who, contented with knowing the truth, lived for himself in a circle of formal duties, wearisome and fruitless of blessing. Some long stalks of the gladiola, that had ceased to flower, and had been cut down, lay beneath my hand, like dead sticks. Hardly knowing what I did, I plaited the reeds together, until they formed a long wand ; and holding it beneath the falling fountain, it divided at its source into three or four little fan-like streams, laving the scorched roots of the plants nearest to it, and sprinkling the dry leaves and fading blossoms with thousands of dew-drops, sparkling in the sunlight as it gleamed in golden rays at intervals through the close, leafy barren of the dark cypress-trees. All at once I realized the comfort that the Holy Spirit alone can impart, — that the work of a bruised and broken reed, in the Hand of Power. can perform whatsoever the maker of that bruised and broken reed appoints.

With delight I watched the sparkling waters led into new currents by my weak hand; when suddenly a rainbow spanned the basin, and my fingers were gathered into its radiant-colored arch. I remembered the faithful Promiser who had led me through the wilderness and brought me safely through the sea, and I adored my gracious Teacher. who in a parable of nature had shown me things to come.

That morning I had been specially led out in prayer for my kinsfolk ; and when, refreshed by my heavenly lesson, I returned to the house, it was to find that the Lord had not forgotten my feeble prayer.

It is difficult not to desire more health and strength than the Lord appoints. Many shattered vessels know that when they reach a certain point of restoration, it is soon at an end, and that they return to the same state. Perhaps there is no earthly blessing that it seems so allowable to plead for as health and strength to perform the service for which we believe we have been peculiarly fitted. But if not a hair of your head can fall without his permission, so not one pain can rack the body dear to its Creator without his will. Pain and helplessness can never really put you anywhere that you can serve Him better than that shady place where He watches over the gold in his furnace.

When we remember the large amount of what is

called work which is unfruitful here, and how much
will be burned up, we see that in the end much outward service has little issue. Many who are laid by
only for a time, maybe only for recollection and refresh-
ing, will learn that waiting is preparation ; and when the
set time is come, the prayer of faith shall raise up the
sick, and show forth the power of the Good Physician,
and the healed servant will exclaim, " It is good to
wait on thee."

I knew a farmer's wife who, like many other hidden
ones of God, was little accounted of in the village
where she was born, and where she had dwelt from
childhood, externally one of the loveliest, and inter-
nally one of the darkest valleys in England. She
was always feeble and sickly, and unable to enter
into the active duties that devolve on a farmer's wife.
Perhaps had it been otherwise with her, the service to
which the Lord had designed her might not have been
so fully accomplished. She was not so rich in this
world's goods as if she had been a hard-working
woman, but in the end she was rich in faith, giving
glory to God. Years had gone by without any faithful
messenger of God sending forth the invitation of the
Heavenly Father to his prodigals, or telling forth the
joys of salvation in that remote village. It was not
then as now, when the good news of salvation sounds
forth in every hamlet in our island.

The death of an aged clergyman, who had left the
people in the same dead calm in which he had found
them in his youth, made way for a young and accomplished student to the vacant cure. His thoughts were

absorbed in his studies and literary pursuits, and in the calm retreat allotted to him, his Greek and Hebrew and botanical researches absorbed his time ; his Sunday service once concluded, his days were spent in theological discussions or current literature of the day ; and as he had no experimental knowledge of that which he had been' sent to teach, the gospel of Jesus Christ was only presented in eloquent words in the pulpit, but sufficed not to reach a scattered and very poor and ignorant neighborhood, called a parish.

So time went on. One day as the young man stood at his door, hat in hand, to proceed on an excursion, he was confronted by a pale, bowed-down woman, whom he supposed to be an applicant for some pecuniary assistance. He politely accosted her, and inquired what he could do for her. With a quiet smile she replied, " Nay, sir, I know not what you can do for *me;* but I thought as the shepherd did not look after his sheep, that it was time at least for the sheep to look after the shepherd."

Then followed the faithful rebuke and warning ; and accompanying him to his little library, the message the Lord had sent by his messenger was told forth in simplicity and power. That day was the turning-point of the young vicar's life. None knew whence that great transformation arose, and he who went to teach remained to learn. He was a slow learner in comparison to one who had been taught of God ; however, he became the instrument of the faith and prayer of this faithful woman.

She told me of the peculiar blessing bestowed on her

the morning she went forth to do her Master's bidding,
to preach the gospel of Jesus Christ to the new incum-
bent. Unasked, the Lord gave her a promise of healing from a disease pronounced incurable, which for
many years had prevented her from walking beyond the
precincts of the farm, and which had rendered the
journey from the hamlet to the vicarage almost impossible, and though in faith she commenced it, she shrank
in dismay from the painful and distressing undertaking.

She had not proceeded above a quarter of the distance, when, asking for strength to accomplish her
task, immediate healing was promised her, and this
not as an answer to prayer, but *gratuitously* offered by
the Great Healer, as if to seal her commission on the
important errand, and enable her to accomplish the
service to which she was ordained. She was never
anything more than a feeble, ailing woman, but from
that day she could undertake many duties hitherto
impossible, and she was healed of her infirmity.

She told me that the promise was given her with
such distinct power, that she looked around to see if
any one had overheard her groan and prayer; but the
birds on the hedge-row were the only witnesses, and
when it was a second time repeated, she walked on
and found she was healed.

In that little study of the young preacher, there
was no guest so welcome as this hidden witness; and
the meek surrender of the pastor's will to the knowledge of the " more excellent way " knit a bond of
affection and sympathy between them, intensified on
his side as he entered into the practical experiences

of the riches of the inheritance for those who desired to know Him whom they believe. The sheep had looked after the shepherd, and had indeed led the shepherd to look after his sheep with a deeper knowledge of their wants — and his own. This was a hidden witness, for none knew the life of faith that sustained her little household, and how often in the times of drought and storm, her only refuge proved to be the Arms ever open to succour and deliver. And this woman, often on her face before the Lord for failure, and for the hidden things to be revealed to her thirsty soul, had to watch for their daily need, and strive to set before her husband the faith and hope which sustained her. So often is it, that the Lord must touch his children on the point most obvious to themselves and others, to trust Him fully for that which they cannot see, but which He calls on them to believe.

Things had gone very sadly at the farm, and faith was tried to the utmost. The hidden witness knew not then that this was the answer to her prayers for a more practical faith for her husband. At last the day came when faith had to be proved to the uttermost : even bread for their daily need failed, and at the breakfast hour, when the farmer returned from the fields for his early meal, the table was certainly spread. but no bread was there. While he was laboring in his field, she was laboring at the Throne of Grace ; and she strove to share with him the hope which now animated her. that though no bread was there, the Lord had surely heard her cry and would help.

The irritation of her husband and his doubt of her

prayer bringing help only sent her to her knees again.
Still there was no bread, and he was very hungry.
With all their losses and trouble, they had never been in
debt, and never so low before ; but now what was to be
done? The dairy had a few cheeses, but the fair was
now at hand, and not one could be touched without
loss.

"If Johnson would only pay me what he owes me,"
said the farmer, " we should get along until fair-day,
for we are safe for the sale of our cheese : but it's all in
vain. I have left off asking for the money. There's
no help for it." he continued sadly, as he sat down to
the table, "fetch the cheese ; we *must* cut it." She
did not move toward the dairy. He followed her with
a reproachful look. "Wait," said the woman who
watched unto prayer,—"wait ; let me tell the Lord that
no help has come"; and she entered again into her
closet. When she left it the cheese was on the table,
— the cheese, the pride of her dairy, but as yet un-
touched. She stayed her husband's hand raised to cut
it, saying, "Wait, I see a man in the barley-field yon-
der. I am sure he is bringing us help." The little
homestead lay on the outskirts of the hamlet, where no
one would come save to and fro to the house. The
farmer rose from his chair, and looking in the direction
that his wife pointed, he exclaimed, "It is Johnson!"

So it was. Breathing hard from his hurried walk,
the man made his way through the yard, as if on some
desperate errand, and almost speechless, laid thirty
shillings on the table. Yes, it was Johnson ; prayed out
of his house, and brought miles at this early hour, with

his conscience touched to the quick by the dealings of the Lord with him, — dealings better known and understood by the farmer's wife than to himself. He looked on the empty plates and the uncut cheese, and confusion covered his face while he said, " I know how long I have owed you this money. I have been using it instead of giving it to you. Some days since I could well have repaid it, but I did not intend to give it to you yet. I hired a horse yesterday to put in our car, to take my wife and children to the sea-coast for a few days. In the night the horse fell sick, and we feared he would die before morning, and I had to send him back ; and I have been so miserable ever since early dawn about this money ! I could not rest till fair-day, when I meant to give it back to you ; but I have brought it over myself, and there it is."

Sometimes these tangible answers are sent for our own weak faith, or the unbelief of others, while long waiting in patience and hope is called for in the reception of the spiritual blessing, invisible to our natural sense. Satan's aim is always to make us mistrustful of God. He brings before us our unworthiness, our faint, broken prayer that seems to *us* no prayer at all ! Yet some homely or simple request, which the formalist thinks too mean to bring before the King of kings, fills the soul of the child of faith with praise and gladness, and enables him to go forward in *His* name, who performeth ALL things for us ! So we go from strength to strength, desiring after and seeking for those precious things which are not seen immediately, but as surely ours as the daily bread and the daily mercies which we so often accept as our natural right.

The work of faith and labor, of love and patience, of hope, will ever be a witness to his glory to all who turn from idols to serve the living and true God, and to wait for his Son from heaven.

The farmer's wife had excused herself from outward testimony, and contented herself with praying, because she felt she was neither believed in nor comprehended. Prayer without testimony had failed, and now she was forced into the position by the power of the Lord, whom she desired to serve in *his* appointed way. The weakness of her body, her great infirmity, her natural timidity, her ignorance, seemed a forcible plea for leaving the learned student alone with his books. But she had been faithful in her constant longing after the souls around her, and the faithful Master would not let her escape a service and lose the blessing he had ordained her.

It was in vain to say, "Behold, O Lord God, I cannot speak, for I am a child." His reply was written long ago : " Say not, I am a child : for thou shalt go to all that I shall send thee, and whatsoever I command thee thou shalt speak. Be not afraid of their faces : for I am *with* thee to deliver thee " (Jer. i. 7, 8) ; and as the power of the Lord prepared Jeremiah for his service, so will He also prepare all whom He calls to a position unsought, undesired, and for which no natural aptitude has been given.

The Holy Spirit began to work in the soul of more than one aged sinner in the village, and many manifest tokens of his power it was given her to behold before she entered into her rest. Deeply was she mourned, and by none more than by the pastor whose life of ease and self-indulgence had been transformed into that of one "who careth for the poor." None knew how the change was wrought in his heart, or how long one of the hidden ones of God had stood between the living and the dead, unrecognized and unvalued by all but Him.

Dear prisoners of the Lord, hidden with Him in his pavilion, hidden in Him in the secret of his presence, hidden in Christ and *abiding* in Him, — be content to be misapprehended, misunderstood; you cannot *enjoy* the earthly, if your spiritual faculties are exescised on the heavenly. But they are being prepared for that enjoyment, for the service of the upper sanctuary, eternal fellowship with those who have washed their robes and made them white in the "blood of the Lamb." "Be patient therefore, brethren, unto the coming of the Lord. Behold, the husbandman waiteth for the precious fruit of the earth, and hath long patience for it, until he receive the early and latter rain." (James v. 7.) When the mourning bride was weeping for him from whom she had wandered, the watchman smote her and wounded her: they knew not Him whom she was seeking, nor his matchless worth, so neither could they understand and respect the grief that overwhelmed her for the loss of her beloved, — a grief that all the watchmen in Zion could neither comprehend nor relieve!

Job's three miserable comforters, had neither spiritual insight nor sympathy to enter into the sufferings of the man *they* condemned, whom the Lord had not condemned. When Stephen did great miracles among the people, false witnesses arose and stoned him; and though his face was as an angel's in brightness, and they listened to his sermon, they hated him still, and that hatred grew for the vision of glory accorded him; for he, by the revelation of the Spirit. beheld what *they* could not see and therefore would not believe. And when Jesus Christ, Son of God, Son of man, came teaching and healing and blessing, shunning neither the feast of the Pharisee, nor the touch of the leper, nor the tears and kisses of the sinner, men scorned and mocked and crucified Him. He was the scorn of the vile, and the song of the drunkard.

There is no Scripture record that can teach us more clearly the value of human favor, than when the Lord began to teach in the synagogue (Luke iv. 22-27): " All bare him witness, and wondered at the gracious words that proceeded out of his mouth"; but ere his discourse had closed, they rose up and thrust him out of the city, and led Him unto the brow of the hill whereon the city was built, that they might cast Him down headlong.

And so it will ever be even unto the end. The wisdom of God and the power of God and the arm of the Lord can only be revealed by the Holy Spirit. When Paul performed the cure on the cripple, the beholders would have sacrificed to him and Barnabas, as heathen gods; but when the apostles reproved the people, and preached to them to turn from their vanities to the living God, they were quickly persuaded to stone them.

Nature can only love nature's fruit, unless it be in harmony with man's requirements, as honesty, meekness, generosity, and such like. How then can the blind of this world discern between things that differ, and know the rules and regulations of life hid with God,— springing from One whom no human knowledge can fathom, that has no beginning or end?

The pillar of cloud sheltered the people of Israel by day, and gave light to them by night; but it was an impenetrable darkness to their enemies, and so it is now. How certain are we that when the world judges the Lord's dealings and the Lord's ways, they will misjudge them and also his people! "God giveth not account of any of his matters" Noah was uncomprehended when he was building the ark, and counted a fool. Moses thought his brethren would understand that he would deliver them when he smote the Egyptian ; but the time was not yet, and they only regarded him as a murderer. Joseph's brethren hated him because of the dreams he had dreamed, foretelling his greatness from the favor of God, when the hand of the Lord was moving for the shepherd-boy, in another manner than for his brethren.

"Behold, the dreamer cometh," marked Joseph's doom ; but the hatred of his brethren was but part of the mighty design to bring him to the place appointed. The priest Eli harshly rebukes the weeping Hannah ; then she poured forth her grief in broken words that reached not human understanding "How long wilt thou be drunken? put away thy wine from thee," is the unpriestly salutation of the unsympathetic man ; yet the woman of sorrowful spirit was telling forth her trouble into the ear of Him mighty to save. The half-uttered sentences, the bursting heart, the falling tear, the smothered sobs, were forcible arguments with the Lord God Almighty. He heard and answered. When David in obedience to his father goes to the field where his first exploits were ordained, his brethren accuse him of motives of pride. " I know thy pride, and the naughtiness of thy heart." (1 Sam. xvii. 29.) Little they knew of the stripling whom God had called separate from his brethren.

Be of good comfort, for He who was with them is with you, and He has said, " If ye were of the world, the world would love his own : but because ye are not of the world, but I have chosen you out of the world, therefore the world hateth you." (John xv. 19.) " The servant is not greater than his Lord." How great would be our loss if we fled from every cross, or if we were saved from every sorrow and difficulty ! How little testimony could we give of his power and his care and his love, if we were defended from every rough breeze that tossed our frail bark, on those stormy billows where He has appeared in our fourth watch, when every earthly hope and expectation had perished ! He is the Lord our " God, that divided the sea, whose waves roared : the Lord of hosts is his name." (Is. li 15.) He might have saved his dear disciples from the storm, but how great would have been their loss — and ours !

He that opened the eyes of the blind could have caused that Lazarus should not have died ; but the tears He shed were to comfort millions of bruised and broken hearts, and the sympathy of the Man of Sorrows at the sepulchre of Bethany sheds to-day over the mourner's heart the balm that takes knowledge of the presence of One acquainted with grief.

All the varied operations of the Holy Spirit draw us to a closer examination of the only safe record that remains intact through ages, — the Word of God. If this revelation of God could be received and comprehended by the natural intelligence, it would not be a divine revelation, and long since it would have been exhausted or destroyed. He who indited its wondrous pages can alone interpret it. It would not defy science or learning if natural research could fathom its mysteries. The eyes and the ears and the heart of the spiritual man are the medium of the Holy Spirit's communication.

Ages roll on, and the divine record only proves its divine origin and the impossibility of its destruction.

The heavenly science can only be comprehended by men of faith who walk in the light, children of the day; how then can it be explained by blind men who walk in the night? If then the mysteries of faith can only be received and accepted and enjoyed by the household of faith, how shall the life that springs from the belief of its veracity be comprehended by the alien? "For that which is highly esteemed among men, is abomination in the sight of God." (Luke xvi. 15.) Why is the Bible more and more valued as we study it? Because we know it is true. Because the voice of him who spake by the prophets now speaks to *us*.

Because we see God in all, and because in these last days God hath. " spoken unto us by his Son," and there we shall daily learn the lesson set forth for our instruction. None else save " the great cloud of witnesses " could bear the continual inspection of their recorded life. without exciting criticism on our part and loss on theirs ; and yet the more we read and ponder on *God's way* with them, it increases our zeal and ardor and reverence and praise.

None can write a man's life save the Holy Spirit. His brother man knows nothing but what he sees, or that he imagines *might be*, or what is or is not in harmony with it ; and thus he makes it an unreal thing. The spiritual man delivered from the body would not recognize his own portrait. A friend could not bear to record the evil, and would exaggerate the good. An enemy would soil what was beautiful and sully what was fair, and magnify the evil. Man cannot write his own life : much he will never tell. though he may write sincerely ; much he cannot tell because it involves the life of others ; much he knows not how to write, and much he is not allowed to write : for there is in every life, *lived out*, secret things that belong alone unto the Lord our God. Yet every man's life is as surely written above as is that of Moses, from his bulrush cradle to his mysterious sepulchre on Pisgah ; as David's, the man after God's own heart, with his harp and his crown, his sins and his sorrows and his prayers and his praise. God *has* written my life and your life, and God's dear Son with his precious Blood hath cleansed that record white as driven snow.

Who that has once found the word of God, as the sword of the Spirit, as well as the leaves for healing, does not know the rest and enjoyment of turning from the most spiritually indited book on Christ to *the* Book itself? The words became absorbed by the spirit, food for the day's sustenance, medicine for the sick, comfort for the sorrowing, strength for the feeble, and hope for the hopeless. There we can dig for gold and never be disappointed, and there we can gather and lay up treasures for our own use and therefore for others. Here the hidden ones of God feast and none shall make them afraid; and they themselves shall be like a watered garden, and like a spring of water whose waters fail not. Fear not to be misunderstood by those who know not Who sealed the fountain; for He is whispering in the desert places in the garden enclosed, "How much better is thy love than wine, and the smell of thine ointments than all spices!" (Sol. Song iv. 10.)

CHAPTER IV.

WATERS OUT OF THE SMITTEN ROCK.

"I have tau, 'it thee in the way of wisdom; I have led thee in right paths." -- Prov. iv. 11.

"He found him in a desert land, and in the waste howling wilderness; He led him about, He instructed him, He kept him as the apple of his eye." —Deut. xxxii. 10.

"I am the Lord thy God which teacheth thee to profit, which leadeth thee by the way that thou shouldest go." — Is. xlviii. 17.

THE object of life is not, What amount of happiness can I secure in the world, what sorrow can I escape, and what can I achieve? but, How may I learn to apprehend the Lord God? (Jer. iv. 23, 24.) If this knowledge were to be acquired by enjoyment of the things of nature, would He whose name is Love withhold one pleasant possession by which we could attain the same end? No! He would fill up the cup of earth's happiness for His beloved children. He has something better and more enduring for them.

Well He knows that the hearts He has created capable of life's sweetest enjoyments are the most susceptible of keenest suffering, — and yet this is their portion.

Thus the object of the Heavenly Science is to bring us acquainted with Him who will teach us what is in our hearts, and the unsearchable riches in the heart of God. (Heb. xii. 11.) Not solely to wean from the world has he sent the varied trials ; not as the punishment for our deservings, though both these and many more causes might be assigned for the chastening whereof all are partakers : but to bring us into conformity with Christ, and thus enable us to see God. (Matt v. 8.)

If this brief existence were the sum of the believer's hope, how great seems the loss entailed by the sick-room, the days and nights of helpless languishing, the seasons of bereavement, the waiting, the watching, that to outward sight bears no sign of service, only that the Lord declares "He that loseth his life for my sake, the same shall find it" ! And it is to be found even here. Ages of bliss are crowded into a moment of blessing : the smile of his favor, the conscious realization of his acceptance, the special promise, the visitation of the Spirit, the fellowship that hath heights and depths that man has never yet proclaimed, and never will, and comprehended only by those broken utterances breathed within, that carry scarce an echo without. Yea ! the life lost for Jesus' sake shall be found again. He can restore us the years that the locust hath eaten, the canker-worm, the caterpillar, and the palmer worm, his great army, which He sent among us, to chasten us and teach us. For every hour lived out for Christ, a seed is cast into the womb of eternity, that shall germinate and bloom and bear fruit forever.

The eyes blinded with tears, weary with watching, dim with age, can gaze like the eagle on the light beyond, undazzled by the glory of the coming sunrise. Yea, man may gaze where angels veil their faces, before the great mystery of *God with us.*

But if earth's glories gain the ascendancy, or idols wean us from our heavenward march, then will the child of God become weak as other men, deaf to the song of the turtle, blind to the love that yearns ever over him.

Hezekiah, who had trusted in the Lord for deliverance from his enemies, and had been delivered, (oh, how marvellously !) who had pleaded for healing and life, and had been heard and answered by one of the most wonderful signs ever granted to man's feeble faith, falls before the vain glory of the perishable things of earth. When the ambassadors came from afar, where some echo of these marvels had already reached them, they were entertained with the sight of the treasures in the palace of the king : the silver and the gold and the spices and the precious stones and the rare ointment and the " pleasant jewels " and his armory. There was nothing in his house and all his dominions that Hezekiah showed them not. But when he displayed his brazen shields, he told nothing of the faithfulness of the Lord God, whose truth had been his shield and buckler. He opened his store-houses of corn and oil, but said nothing of the miracle of his cure through his pleading and tears ; nothing of the power of prayer with Jehovah ; nothing of the fifteen years added to his life ; nor of the letter spread before him in utter

helplessness, when the Lord of heaven and earth made
the cause his own. When all earthly hopes of deliverance from his mighty enemy had vanished, had he so
soon forgotten the strength and consolation in his distress from the swift response of the Lord? And what
of the defence of the city? and his deliverance out of
the hand of Sennacherib, by the supernatural intervention of the Lord of hosts, of his Angel, who smote in
the camp of the Assyrian an hundred fourscore, and
five thousand men of war in a night, men of valor,
their leaders and captains, ready to come down on the
fenced city, and take captive the people, — but where
were they? Oh, what an opportunity of telling of the
faithfulness of the God of David, the faithful God!
(2 Kings xix. 34.) Hezekiah could display the treasures of his house, and the treasures of his fathers, —
of these doubtless the Babylonians had heard, and seen
things as costly in their own land ; but they had never
heard, from the lips of a king, of the Holy One of
Israel, and the treasures *laid up* for them that love
Him, and who has respect unto the tears and prayers
of a sinful child of Adam, *because* the Lord is pitiful
and of tender mercy. True, some may have mocked,
but *one* may have believed. Some, astonished at these
marvels of grace, *may* have questioned, Can such
things be? and have carried to their people in the far-
off land some glorious facts of the God of Israel, —
the God of Hezekiah ! But it was not so.
. The hand of the Lord is seen, as we so often perceive it, in falling on the idol that has obscured his
glory, and silenced the witness of his love and power.

The treasures laid up on earth were carried away to those very people to whom they had been proudly displayed, because God was not acknowledged in them; and the treasures of heavenly grace that might have been set forth by the recipient were disposed for the empty admiration and presents of strangers, even for Babylon! Doubtless Hezekiah thought for such a letter there was no necessity to spread it before the Lord, as he had done that of the ambassador of Sennacherib. The treasures and possessions in his dominions were not seen in a day, so that dwelling in the atmosphere of admiration of strangers, he forgot the shield of his salvation; and it was in love that the Lord allowed him to learn what was in his heart.

Cannot we recall many such losses in the life of faith, when the Lord has allowed some Babylonian ambassador to arrive suddenly before us to inquire of our welfare, with a letter? We might have spoken of him, who had done such great things for us, yet we were content to leave the service of the sanctuary, to meet strangers on their own ground, either from love of approbation or vanity, or because we have thought it unlikely that they could enter into the interest of spiritual things. Grateful for their natural kindness, we have acknowledged it in their own fashion, and lost our true standing-point outside the camp. Possibly they might not have reciprocated our witnessing of the living God, " the Saviour of all men, specially of those that believe." but what is that to us? our service is the same before God, " Magnify the word that men behold." Men may behold it afar off. What is it to us, if stran-

gers go forth from us admiring our natural gifts? *that*
will not attract the heart to the imperishable treasures
hid in Christ Jesus ; on the contrary, the thoughts will
be occupied by the very things which have caused us to
stumble, and will obscure his glory, which surely is the
chief aim of the child of God   Envy and jealousy
may exaggerate our possessions, and covet *them*.
What harm could it do us, if we *had* told them of the
power and the love of God, his wonderful dealings on
our behalf, and they *had* derided us? or we had told
them of his marvels exhibited to us, and they *had* disbelieved?   O dear brethren! what is that to us, in
comparison to the joy that fills the soul of the child of
the Kingdom when he follows the Lord through good
report and evil report?   " Labor not for the meat that
perisheth. but for that meat which endureth unto everlasting life."   (John vi. 27.)

Hearts do not always express in face or voice any
symptom of receiving, but God only sees the heart,
and knows how much conscience may writhe, when pride
seals the lips.   One whose soul was exercised by the
Spirit. in anguish of heart sought a Christian friend,
who she expected would counsel her and help her in
the way of salvation, — a way of which she was ignorant, yet longing to find the Saviour of whom she
had heard.   The lady was busy surrounded with plans
for a house she was building ; these she exhibited,
pointing out the alterations and amendments she con-
templated on the architecture.   The cultivated taste of
her visitor led her to desire her approval.   She would
once have entered into this with zest ; now she longed for

Jesus. The sorrowful soul waited long for an opening to speak of her misery. But the sad countenance and trembling voice did not reach the heart of the lady, engrossed in the beauty of the house which she was projecting. The Lord had sent a messenger to her to hear of the grace that had saved *her*, the mercy that had encompassed *her*, and the loving-kindness awaiting every one that sought his face. The sorrowful soul did not perish: long after, one of the little ones of the flock pointed her to the Blood, the " precious Blood of Christ, as of a lamb without blemish and without spot," and she realized at last pardon and peace; but oh, the lost blessing from seeking the things that are seen, and watching not for the things that are not seen and which are eternal!

Without the trials of our way our eternal inheritance becomes like a myth, and loses that practical individual power and interest in our every-day life. Our loins become loosely girded, our sandals unbraced, and our sword rests in the scabbard, unfitted for lack of use to the warfare to which the Captain of our salvation has called us. And often, why? Because we fear the mockery of fools. Jeremiah, forgetting the rich promises of the Lord, said he would speak no more because he was mocked; but the fire burned within, and it burned up the fear and the shrinking (Jer. xx. 9); he was weary of forbearing, and he again went forth as the messenger of the Lord to kings and people, and prophesied of that Righteous Branch " who shall reign and prosper, and shall execute judgment and justice on the earth "

Let us not take our lessons in the school of God as

punishments from a hard taskmaster. Large sums are paid for perfectionary lessons in art, and often it is considered as a boon even then to receive a pupil. And what is it after all? The hand that holds the pencil will soon stiffen and grow cold, and what does it leave behind? Only perishable treasures. Lips that have learned to charm thousands in sweetest strains, and hands that have drawn forth entrancing music, if they have not been tuned to his praise will sink again to the earth, for the praise for which alone they labored. Yet no one is heard to complain of the time they must give to the consideration of such lessons, or the amount paid for the acquirements. Yet how we murmur when the Lord of the whole earth condescends to teach us for *Eternity!* Granting that *his* lessons cost tears and pains and money, perhaps half our fortune, or the whole, perhaps years of sickness, disappointment, rejection. — yet the lessons are designed for eternity in the Heavenly Science, a knowledge of the great I AM. How thankful should we be (and we shall be when we see as we are seen) to pay with tears and pains and earthly possessions for this knowledge that maketh wise unto salvation, which has led us to *know Him* who has loved us with an everlasting love! " No man should be moved by these afflictions, for yourselves know that we are appointed thereunto." (1 Thess. iii. 3.)

The prophecies that came aforetimes to nations and individuals are no less recorded to show forth the power and faithfulness of God, than to make known to us the way in which the prophets themselves were continually prepared for instruments of the service to which they were called. The minute care of God for the perfecting of his instrument is no less needed for our instruction individually than his promises and threatenings and warnings to his often rebellious and backsliding people of old, to whom the prophets were first sent. Take, my brethren, the prophets who have spoken in the name of the Lord, for an example of suffering, affliction, and patience. The faith and patience of Jeremiah is one of our examples of the blessing given to those who believe, against all the convictions of sense, and all the temptations of the agents of Satan to shake their faith.

The patriarchs and prophets were men of like passions as ourselves, men of sign, though they recognized it not, shrinking from their office, alike poor in spirit, and unconscious fully of the power of the divine mission intrusted to them. I heard a preacher enjoin his hearers to seek for self-possession in delivering the message of salvation. I know not if they did so, or if they obtained it. It seems to me the most powerful instruments in the Lord's hands have been broken pitchers, bruised reeds, and ram's horns. Isaiah, Jeremiah, Ezekiel had continual need of encouragement, and were continually taught by suffering that which they had to declare to others. They had no consciousness of possessing anything apart from the Spirit that imbued them ; as men of sign they could not understand that which could only be received by faith, and that which was to come hereafter. They feared, though the Lord was evidently with them and appeared to them to

assure them of his presence and favor. Yet Isaiah
was desolate from his conscious uncleanness when the
Lord drew nigh, so that he felt unfit for the office to
which he was called; and Jeremiah, from ignorance and
weakness, shrank from the service that had been appointed him   We have all these as teachers in the
school.   And the great lack of Christians is a fuller
belief in the word of God, taken as a revelation to his
church and to us individually.   The words spoken to
Noah, Moses, Isaiah, Jeremiah, are for me.   The words
from the lips of my blessed Lord at Bethany, at Sychar,
on the mountain, in the desert, on the sea, in the synagogue, everywhere, are for *me*, as if spoken to-day.
The epistles of Paul to the churches, to Timothy,
Peter's heart-searching, sifting, and John's loving con-
straint, all as if newly written and indited by the Holy
Comforter to myself.   The Proverbs of Solomon are as
goads and nails in my armor, though written out of
the abundance of his gift to all sorts and conditions of
men.   The groans and sighs and complaints of Job are
for my edification ; and David's harp was tuned for my
praise, my woe, my conflicts, my deliverances from the
oppression of my enemies, my nights of weeping, and
my gladness of heart.

It is not a life of sense that we have to cultivate, but
the life of *faith*, by which the Lord is to be glorified.

Was there no preparation of the man chosen *before*
his birth, and set apart as a messenger for the great
and mighty God?   Jeremiah was not chosen because of
his power, when he urged against his call, "Ah, Lord
God, I cannot speak, for I am a child."   He felt his

utter inability for the service, and the Lord deals with him as one shrinking and helpless; He comforts and encourages and warns him, and strengthens his timid servant by visible signs to shadow forth the invisible, — the rod of the almond-tree and the seething-pot. The same promise is given to all whom the Lord calls to serve and follow him, is never withheld from his chosen servant to-day. *I am with thee.*" (Gen. xxvi. 24; Gen. xxviii. 15.)

He had called him by name. He had promised him his presence as He had done aforetime to the patriarchs, to Moses, to Joshua. (Joshua i. 59.) Will He give less to-day to those whom He bids to the field and to the battle? In vain is the man sent of God imprisoned. Harmless fell the accusation against him as a false prophet and deceiver. Vain are the rage and malice of his enemies against the man who had no earthly defence, but whose fortress was the living God, who had declared, "They shall fight against thee, but they shall not prevail against thee, for *I am with thee*, to deliver thee." The messenger of God, who would have excused himself from service, was made by the word of the Lord only, "A defenced city, an iron pillar, a brazen wall against the whole land," against the kings of Judah, against the princes thereof, and against the priests thereof, and against the people. Is it not worth the cup of suffering drank with the Saviour, to do his bidding, to carry his message, whether it be the needful warning or the promise of blessing, whether you be accepted or whether it is rejected?

The feet of the man of sign are sunk in the mire, the

sign of that which metaphorically awaited the cruel king.
(Jer. xxxviii. 22)   The warning must be given. the
message must be delivered, whether in the court of the
house of the Lord. or in the prison. or the palace
of kings.   The word of the Lord came to Jeremiah,
after long waiting. and the word of the Lord can reach
us. and the service He has ordained for us can be
accomplished wherever we may be, and under whatsoever persecution ; if only we can take our stand as
his servants. willing to fulfil his design, then we can
answer in the words of the Master, "Thou couldst
have no power at all against me, except it were given
thee from above." (John xix. 11.)   The purchase of
the field by the right of inheritance and redemption was
a special act of faith in the imprisoned prophet (Jer.
xxiii. 7) ; and although involving the interest of the
nation, yet as a family transaction it holds a peculiar
place in the life of the *man*, and yet bearing on the future
of the Jewish nation.   The recorded prayer that follows the completion of the purchase bears no similarity
to his timid appeal when he shrinks from the mighty
task awaiting him.   "O Lord God, behold I cannot
speak, for I am a child." (Jer. i. 6.)   Now he knows
Him as the great, the mighty God, the Lord of hosts,
great in counsel and mighty in work. and can urge.
"Is *anything* too hard for Thee?" for, dwelling on
the wonders of the past, he can trust the Lord to-day.
And what has brought this mighty change ?   He was
already sanctified from the womb, and ordained to the
work to which he was called.   But the Lord had yet
to put his word in the mouth of the shrinking man.

even as on the day of Pentecost the fiery tongues from heaven sent forth those unlearned men, who had spoken to and listened to the Lord Himself, who had "handled the word of life."

The first message that Jeremiah carried to Jerusalem is one of tender pleading, peculiarly suited to his sympathetic character. He pleads as a husband deserted by his bride, as a mother bereaved of her children, as if the natural tenderness of his nature should be used in this first appeal to his beloved people.

The prophet was a man of sign, but as the messenger of God he must be a faithful and obedient servant. God has shown us that the man He had chosen was not elected for his gifts and energy. His nature shrank from the task of condemnation, and he would find no satisfaction in denouncing the wickedness and rebellion against the Lord who sent him; showing that the Lord can make use of nature's gifts, or leave them entirely aside and often disprove that such gifts are needful "He giveth wisdom to the wise, and to them that have no might He increaseth strength; but this is not the strength of nature, nor the wisdom of the wise of this world."

The strength of the prophet was in the word of the Lord; that word stands forever, and speaks to us to-day, as to Jeremiah. Jehudi cut up the roll whereon it was written and cast it into the fire; and though it was consumed on the hearth, the word of the Lord remains the same to-day. "It is written," the same as when Jeremiah uttered it, and Barak wrote it! "Thus saith the Lord" remains for us, for all ages.

Men with unholy hands may mutilate and disfigure its
fair proportions, but what God has said remains forever. The promises and the power that sustained the
patriarchs and prophets and apostles are for us to-day
our unalterable possessions, more precious for the use
of ages that proved them as gold is proved.

Jeremiah must needs be in "the court of the prison"
to deliver his message; it was not his unfaithfulness
that sent him there for chastisement, but his faithfulness, and the glorious messages which this messenger
of God had to deliver must oftentimes have strengthened his own heart in faith of that Blessed One, who
had been the shield and buckler of his life when hated
by those to whom he was sent as the prophet of the
nation. It is confidence in the love and power and
faithfulness of God that is honored by Him.

The weakness and ignorance of the apostles even
while the Lord was with them are a convincing proof of
the power of the Holy Ghost. The *promise of the
Father*, which was to send them forth in boldness to
witness for the Lord, was expected, prayed for, waited
for, — and received. Here was the secret of blessing, —
his name; faith in that name worked miracles, and
therefore by the hands of the apostles were many signs
and wonders wrought amongst the people. Thus
"with great power gave the apostles witness of the
resurrection of the Lord Jesus, and great grace was
upon them all, so when the Lord called his apostle Paul
of the Gentiles to witness for Him, the declaration of
his favor was inscribed on his message: "I will show
him what great things he must suffer for my name's

sake." "Surely if we lived near the Lord, we should not require such perpetual chastening?" inquired one. I know not; God and the soul exercised can alone answer that question, and whether it be under the head of " chastisement " our sufferings are upon us. If a father sent his son on a long journey, which entailed much privation and even personal danger, to search out a tract of land in his dominion and to discover mines there which should hereafter be his property, the hardships the son may have to endure can hardly be called punishment. And what shall we say of those who bore no very evident testimony of life in Christ, and who pass away without any special mark of the Refiner's fire? were they so far perfected that they needed it not?

We must see suffering in another light before we can accept it in love and reverence. The Lord knows his own. He knows that the cup He gives will be apportioned to the strength He waits to bestow. The glory of God in these poor, frail temples, indwelt by the Holy Spirit, is seen by their being able to withstand their great Enemy in the power of his might, the same power of the same Divine Person who sustained the Chief Shepherd, who went before his flock in the path He has ordained them to tread. *He knows* that affliction is " grievous," He has declared it, and the Angel of his presence saved *them*, — it will save *us*. We must *wait* for the peaceable fruit of righteousness ; for He has promised it, and they that wait on Him shall not be ashamed.

We need much consideration on this momentous fact of our education for eternity. We must not regard

it as an abstract, individual theory, but as the arena
of the triumphs of Christ, and the glory of God.
Our reflections ought not always to return to "How
much I suffer and how little I can do!" but How much
can I enter into the purpose of my Lord and Master in
this affliction?" When the vine-dresser prunes the vine it
weeps, both before its fruit is formed and after the fruit
is seen; and when the heart is wounded, the tears will
flow, whether we have known the touch of the pruning-
knife one year or ten years. Happy it is that they
do; for the Lord does not prune dead branches, but
living, fruit-bearing ones.

The question arises, How are we to profit by affliction, the purpose of which is not revealed? We pray for
instruction, but we do not pray for intelligence in our
affliction and perplexity to apprehend the Lord, his will
and purposes in the peculiar trials of faith, and we become as it were estranged from Him. But it is not
really so. He is not estranged from us. The wondrous union of soul and mind and body will keep the
child of God at such seasons in conscious weakness,
often with cloud and fear, — an earthen vessel to be
filled with a divine flame. Can there be clouds, if we
abide in Him?

The disciples were with Jesus when under a cloud,
and though it was a "bright cloud," they feared.
Bright, because the love of the Father fell through it
upon the Son with whom He was well pleased; and now
in the cloud that overshadows us, love makes it bright
for his sake, because we are in Him. We may well fear
to hear only the voice of God, because the cloud,

though bright, is still a cloud, and we shrink and trem-
ble under it. We must hear the voice of Jesus our
Redeemer, before we can have confidence to lift up our
eyes and see Him, and Him only.

> "Arise! with Him is safety,
>   With Him is life and light;
>   Wait for Him, though He tarry
>   Till the fourth watch of the night."

We need contact with Him, as when He touched
Daniel, and said unto him, "Fear not, O man greatly
beloved! Be strong, yea, be strong!"

Yes! He knows that we are dust, and that though
He has been with us up the mountains and in the desert
and on the wild sea, we fail to recognize the Lord who
loves us, Father, Friend, and God. That the flood and
the furnace is the portion of the Lord's witnesses, all
know who know themselves as his. We ask for deliverance out of it, or protection from it; but how seldom,
when the darkness has gathered round us, and we cannot see, do we trust Him in the shadow of his wing, or
allow the billows to break over us without fighting
against them! (2 Cor. iv. 7.)

From a life of tribulation which is now fast drawing
to its close, I declare that the trials of our faith, even
through the heaviness of manifold temptations, is among
the most precious marks of a Saviour's love; more
rich in instruction, more suitable for keeping alive our
spiritual energies, and more useful to our fellow men
than years of intellectual service, beheld by the world
and lauded by the church. "They that go down to the

sea in ships, that do business in great waters, these see
the works of the Lord and his wonders in the deep."
The gospel of the Kingdom is preached by every iso-
lated member of the flock, who lives the life of faith in
the living God; by the bedridden pauper full of the
Spirit; by the decrepit man, or the poor woman with
her large and increasing family, who live the life of
faith. Such dealing with a personal Saviour may draw
on them the ridicule, or at most the wonder of the
neighborhood in which they dwell; yet they are setting
forth and witnessing for God, as fully as many an evangelist who speaks his thoughts on a text. It is true
that the hearers may not be so many nor the emotion
so evident; but it may also be considered that all listen-
ers may not be recipient. nor the fruit abiding. The
living faith of many a silent preacher is influencing the
atmosphere of his dwelling-place, unconsciously to himself. Let us praise the mighty power of God, who is
sending forth his army, whether in rank or file or
single combatant. But let us not dwell only on what
is evident to the carnal man. but acknowledge his heav-
venly agents everywhere where the Holy Spirit can
dwell. Let us remember to bless Him for those hidden
members of the body who glorify Him in the fires, and
preach to our heart of a sublimer faith and patience
than we have attained.

There was one of the poor of the flock, so poor that
some questioned if He were really of the Good Shepherd's sheep; as if He who held the whole world in
his hand had not *chosen* the path of peculiar poverty
and trial for peculiar blessing! He gathers the fruit of

his garden, sometimes from one plant and sometimes
from another; his honey and his spikenard, his aloes
and his myrrh, as seemeth good unto Him. Our poor
brother, rich in faith, lived in a little cabin, rent free,
for opening a gate in a branch road in the country,
little frequented; and the pittance he received for it
could not supply him with the necessaries of existence,
which left room for the Lord's hand to be often seen in
his deliverance and blessing. Oftentimes his food consisted of a little oatmeal, and there were days when
even that was less; but the promise of the Everlasting
Father never failed, nor the often trembling faith that
grasped it. To the desolate widow of Sarepta and our
dear gate-keeper the promise was proved every day
new. The barrel of meal shall not waste, neither shall
the cruse of oil fail. God's word shall never be expended, neither the oil of the anointing stay.

Like David, there are days when we cry, " My feet
had wellnigh slipped, but the mercy of the Lord held
me up"; and outwardly, things had gone worse and
worse with our old friend, and it seemed as if the occupation, of which he alone seemed capable, he must soon
leave. One rough night in winter he went to bed, not
expecting to be required to open the gate in that tem-
pestuous night. However, at midnight, he heard the
sound of wheels. He rose instantly, and by the light
of his lantern, he saw a traveller in a gig with a strong,
spirited horse. He passed rapidly through the gate and
was lost in the darkness. Occasionally some trifling
gratuity was given by the passer-by; perhaps he had
expected it would be the case now, in his great extrem-

ity, but it was not given. Never had faith been so
severely tried as this day : but he remembered the past,
and clung to the faithful Friend who had sustained
him marvellously through long years ; and as he laid his
head again upon his pillow, he said, "I can trust Thee
still." It was Sunday morning, and as he opened his
cottage door the morning light fell on a leather portmanteau lying in the road. How came it there? The
traveller of the preceding night must have lost it.
How should he discover the owner and restore it to
him? There was no opportunity of making inquiries
in the neighboring town until the morrow, so he took it
into his care. On Monday morning he set forth to the
town, and before he reached the inn where he hoped to
gain some information of the owner, a large placard
met his eye offering five pounds reward for the recovery
of the portmanteau ; he had only to make the application, and the money was paid him. This seems a
small matter to those who have many five pounds.
But hidden within the hand of the Lord was the thread
of circumstance by which He was about to honor the
faith of his saints. The circumstance brought him in
contact with Christians who knew nothing of the power
of living faith ; and not least the owner of the lost
luggage, who, recognizing a little one of the flock
who glorified his Master in the dark day unseen by
man, was used as the instrument that sustained him for
further visible testimony, to the building up of many
lukewarm believers. It bore another line of instruction to myself. A young student for the ministry, in
whom I felt great interest, heard of the event, and went

himself to speak face to face with the man of faith. New life sprang up in his earnest-hearted, but until then lifeless ministry. The dear old gate-keeper was used of the Lord, instead of a college of learned divines, to send forth a disciple in the power and simplicity of the gospel, to preach of Him of whom he had heard and now had at last seen and handled. "For to love Him with all the heart and all the understanding and all the soul, is more than all burnt-offering and sacrifices."

We must not judge the Spirit's work only by external service, and all that is not of the Spirit but of the might and power of the flesh has no permanence. The silent prayer which has of late years given more life to our public services has perhaps been the most efficacious of all prayer; and there are seasons when we know " the Lord speaketh in his Holy Temple : let all the earth keep silence before Him." In that silence, to the needy and receptive soul there is communion too deep to be realized in the busy rush of the day ; lessons are learned in those seasons, — lessons for ourselves and others, learned for our Father's house, for eternity. Among the many classes in the school of God, sickness has its place ; but true health is that which tends to *life*, a life that cannot be touched by death.

In regard to the question often incautiously advanced, " Why are you not healed? " let us beware that we make not the heart of the righteous sad, whom God hath not made sad, and like Job's miserable comforters' words, condemn with words of truth without knowledge, and counsel without God. " Be ye not unwise, but understanding what the will of the Lord is," has always seemed to me the secret by which alone we can meet the many mysterious difficulties of healing. Without his wisdom how can we understand our own position? Much less can we give the only true sympathy and counsel. in the yet more ardous task of entering into another's. Job's friends had no conception of the testimony for which he was being prepared through a fiery ordeal, a sickness of no common order, his household troubles, his bereavement, his poverty!

A word spoken in season, how good it is! but unless God gives the word, there is more wounding than healing with our willing but unskilful touch; but "a man of understanding shall attain unto wise counsels." (Prov. i. 5.) We do not read that the apostles considered the sick as sinners above all sinners, or Paul, when he wrote to his ailing son in the faith, would certainly have reproved him for being laid aside from work that needed every minister. And when his friend and disciple was left at Miletum sick (2 Tim. iv. 20), he would have used the occasion of warning. In regard to the Corinthian converts, the cause of their affliction was known to Paul, therefore he could say wherefore so many were sickly, and "many sleep." (1 Cor. xi. 29, 30.) Surely if any one could have been expected to be exempt from sickness it would have been Paul himself, for he partook more deeply of the tribulation in the cup which his Lord called him to take from his hand than any who had followed Christ; yet he tells us that "without were fightings and within were fears." Added to his other trials was the "thorn

in the flesh "; its peculiar form is unrevealed to us, and
that to the consolation of many sufferers who cannot
gauge their hidden thorn by that of the apostle of the
Gentiles.   Whatever it was, he besought the Lord
thrice that He would deliver him from it, and received
in reply, "My grace is sufficient for thee," the signifi-
cance of which bears striking similarity of rejoinder to
that of Moses's oft-repeated request, "Speak no more
to me on this matter." (Gal. iv. 15.)   Paul bears witness that the loving disciples in the church of Galatia,
when he had preached Christ among them in the infirmity of the flesh, were ready to pluck out their own
eyes for him, surely pointing to some infirmity of vision ; as also from the fact of several of his epistles having been written for him, which would hardly have been
the case had he been able to write them himself.   It
was the wide field of suffering in which his knowledge
and affections were enlarged and cultivated, the plough-
ing up of a powerful nature in the school of God.
Many have prayed for health who have never found
it.   The Lord had other purposes than theirs in the
class in which He had placed them.   I know intimately
those whose case has been considered hopeless, and
used no means, but submitted meekly to the affliction,
and the Lord has healed them suddenly ; and this in
the midst of peculiar trials and distress, as if a compen-
sating gift for the season of the east wind.   I know
those very near and dear to the Lord, raised for certain purposes from a bed of suffering, and again laid
down when that purpose was accomplished.
    There is no end to the ramification of the uses to

which sickness has been ordained of God. To assert
that He only uses it as a voice of reproof, would be
to wound the tender heart of the Son of Man, in the
person of his sick disciples. He makes our bed in our
sickness. Who comforts us even as a sick child is
comforted of his mother, and who by this means often
keeps this sad season of suffering and solitude the
instruction and revelation of many a mystery long
sought and desired? He knows that the darkness and
the silence and the dew of the night are as needful to his
garden as the morning with its sunlight and balmy air.
Sickness may unfit us for certain forms of service,
which we or our brethren may think indispensable for
the church of Christ; but the work *by* us is of very
little import to the value of the work *in* us, wrought by
the Master's hand, delicately perfecting his instrument
for a more wonderful exhibition of his grace and power
than we can imagine, and which, like some shrouded
sculpture, will be revealed hereafter, to the wonder of
those who have not estimated the *Master* hand in the minute detail of *his* work. It is true the promise to Moses
was, "The Lord will take away from thee all sickness, and
will put none of the evil diseases of Egypt which thou
knowest upon thee"; but we must not part asunder what
God hath joined together, — "*but* will lay them upon
all that *hate thee*." Now we know that it is not so in
this dispensation. We see the enemies of the Lord,
who are our enemies, often free from all diseases, and
not plagued like other men, going on still in paths of their
own evil hearts' choice, while the dearly beloved of the
Lord are serving Him on a couch of pain. "He maketh

his sun to rise on the evil and on the good, and sendeth rain on the just and the unjust." But He goeth *before* his sheep. If we look on the record of the saints of God, we shall see that the tribulation is the portion for his children ; it is not his enemies for whom is reserved the suffering and the pain and the shame. " Be patient therefore, brethren, unto the coming of the Lord. Behold, the husbandman waiteth for the precious fruit of the earth, and hath long patience for it, until he receive the early and latter rain." (James v. 7.) Let patience have her perfect work, for He will come. The hidden life hath its treasures that eye hath not seen nor imagination conceived : that lie like pearls enfolded in unsightly shells, beneath the dark waters, through whose waves we must dive to secure them. They are among the treasures of darkness, and few have the faith to believe they can be found, or possess the courage to work and wait for, and so receive the good things prepared for them that love Him. Be assured of one thing, the *love of God.* Do not think so much of getting free of your cross, whether it be sickness or any other, as being conformed to the will of the Lord, which is conformity to your Saviour. If you have prayed for patience and meekness and love, count it no strange thing that He leads you by paths you have not trodden heretofore.

Everywhere is change, to bring to pass *change* in the soul ; and so it is emptied from vessel to vessel, that the wine may be refined. This is more directly visible to some thoughtful minds than others.

If signs and wonders are to be worked by the Holy

Spirit, and you have called on the Lord to show to
you great and mighty things that you know not, then
pause and ask if He is not revealing them in the cross
He lays upon you.   The prayer of faith must come of
the Holy Comforter, but there is always an answer to
subject prayer ; but an " answer" does not imply that it
will be always according to our natural desire.

Looking away from our *own* loss or gain in the
matter of sickness, how much have we to praise the
Lord for the service of the sick ones of his flock?
Some are laid low to minister to an unbelieving nurse
or doctor ; to break the bread from heaven, and to light
a lamp in the darkness to one who, though rich in
human science and the wisdom of this world, yet has
never seen or known experimentally of the wisdom
that is not of this world, but cometh from above, — perhaps with all his skill unable to fathom the disease, or
do more than release the sufferer for a brief season, and
understanding nothing of the failure of all acknowledged remedies, until the unsearchable mystery of life
shall be solved before the great white throne.

And what shall we say of the changes of climate,
which have sent within the last fifty years noted messengers of good tidings to other climates, to mineral springs,
to mountains where the sound of the everlasting gospel
had never been heard, and where some soul was waiting for the light to a lamp that a dying hand was
appointed to kindle, that should lead many to the feet
of the Lord Jesus?

So from the place of pain the weak and suffering ones,
willing servants of the most high God, go forth, led

by ways they know not, to the sunny coasts of the blue Mediterranean, to the sands of Egypt, to the pine-crowned hills and reviving air of the glaciers, to the temperate clime of New Zealand, and the fruitful valleys of Spain.

It would lift the feeling of loneliness and exile that is experienced by many thus sent forth, if they would take up their cross of sickness and bear it for *His* sake who bore our infirmities and sickness, and who is able and willing to give us strength to uphold and wisdom to direct us ; who can restore health at a word, or carry us through the rough waters and guide us through rough places, better than as a mother careth for her child. (Is. lxvi. 13.) Sickness as well as every other cross *may* have the Voice that woke the soul of the widow of Sarepta to cry to the prophet Elijah, " Art thou come to call my sin to remembrance?" But again, it may be a preparation to declare to the ambassador whom the Lord shall commission to inquire of our welfare, the signs and wonders which the God of Israel works in our midst to-day ; to show forth the tenderness of the Good Physician to his sick ones, and tell of his grace to the wanderers, and his mercies every day new.

Enough if the upright soul makes his request known unto Him, and gives room for the hand of the Lord to work, his voice to be heard, and his foot to be traced. Then shall his promise shine forth as the bow in the cloud : " I will instruct thee, and teach thee in the way which thou shalt go ; I will guide thee with Mine eye."

> "Rise ! let thy garments girded be,
> And listen for the Master's call ;

For 'mid earth's many voices, know
  The Lord's own voice is heard in *all*.
Hear thou instruction, and be wise,
  Watch daily at his gate to learn;
Yea, wait, and by the faith *He gives*,
  His will, his way thou shalt discern.
He is afflicted in thy grief,
  In all thy pain He takes a part;
And draws thee with love's golden cords
  The closer to his tender heart."

Some timid followers of the Lamb are stumbled at healing being set forth as a slumbering gift of the church.
Let us receive the consideration of it with thankfulness.
What is it? *Faith in God*, which has been promised to
move mountains of difficulty. It can renew the suffering body and depressed mind, influenced by the weight
of infirmities and rendered unfit for certain services by
harassing pain and the prostration of sickness.

Healing, whether by the special gift (1 Cor. xii.) of
some in the church, as Dorothea Trüdel, Zeller, and
others, or whether by anointing, according to James v.,
or by some means sanctified by the sick, or even without any means but the faith which believes in the cure,
— such cases are multiplying around us, and it demands
the earnest, believing consideration of individual Christians. Not that the gift has ever been extinct; but so
rarely has testimony been given of the gift of simple
faith that there has been very little evidence of the
power vested in him that believeth. By my own experience I see the same faith is needed to point out a rem-
edy, and the faith of the recipient to *accept* it, as the
prayer without means. Also I have seen, when the

relief from God's word alone was disbelieved in, the disease has returned. Some cases I have had no power to pray for recovery, for I have had the consciousness that it would not be given; and I could see that any means used would increase the disease, and bring no alleviation, and that the patient acceptance of the cross was called for, in which case the Lord has promised, "So far but no farther shall it proceed," for He has set too the bounds thereof. Some have persisted in means, and been met by disastrous consequences; and some have taken up the cross, and borne it in patient meekness, and grown in grace into the beauty of holiness, with a disease arrested by the hand of the Great Healer, and left as a token of his will and power.

I met an interesting and very original woman, who told me she had undergone seven operations for internal disease, and was brought nigh unto death. I knew not what her state was before God, and I said, "That was the Lord, standing at the door, asking you to give your life to Him."

She answered with animation, "Yes, yes, you are right, it was so; but He speaks a different message with every visit. Before the last operation, I awoke my husband early in the morning, and told him that the Lord had said to me that I was not to have that doctor that attended me any more. He replied that it would be a difficult thing to dismiss him in that summary manner, adding, 'Perhaps it is only a dream after all, and there is nothing in it.' 'God has said it,' I replied firmly, 'and I will not have his attendance again.' 'What will you do then?' inquired my husband. 'That I cannot tell you now, but I shall be guided,' I replied." That afternoon, a lady of her acquaintance called upon her, and in the course of conversation mentioned a lady doctor in the city, and urged her at least to consult her, and with such persistency that she consented. As she was leaving the house for this purpose, some friends arrived from the country to pass the day, and her husband endeavored to persuade her to remit her visit to the city for another day, adding, "Any other time will do as well." She said, "I was watching the indication of the Lord's will concerning me, and said, 'I must go now.'"

The doctress would not undertake the case, but mentioned the name of a surgeon recently arrived in the city, and suggested that she should see him at once. The lady drove to the door, and found he had not returned from his visits, but writing a few lines on her card, requested him to call upon her the following day. Accordingly he came and desired a consultation ; and when it was over, he made known to the patient that an operation must take place at once. "Then," said she, "I cast myself into the hands of God, and I said to Him, 'Lord, my soul is Thine, my body is Thine ; take it, do what Thou wilt with it. Thou art the Master ; I am ready to die or live and suffer.' And a deep peace fell upon me. The operation completed, I refused all opiates, and as I lay down I said, ' Lord, let this be the last ! ' and it was so. I was cured." When the surgeon examined the incision, he said to his colleague, " It is a miracle to me : she is healed." However, he told her to lie still for six months ; but when four months had passed, she was on the mountains like the patient of old, walking and praising God. With great energy and earnestness she said, as she ended the history of her cure, " All we have to do is to give ourselves continually into the hands of God, and let Him do all for you without fear. There is nothing else worth living for ; look straight to Him for everything, and keep up a constant communication with Him, and never sleep with anything against anybody. No, go straight to God with it, say, 'They have done wrong, but I will not do wrong.' What pleasure is there but to speak to Him? Ask, seek, knock : for those who ask, receive ; and those who seek, find ; and those who knock, always get the gate open at last." She was entirely relieved of every indication of disease, and her health and strength renewed in a remarkable manner. Naaman *might* have been healed, without bathing in the Jordan, by the word *spoken;* but it was the obedience of faith in Elijah's God which made him descend seven times into the waters of Jordan before he was healed. Thus he knew the God of Israel by his obedience to the word of the prophet. Many seek counsel and light on their way, yet desire their own will in the matter. They say in a manner like Naaman, " Are not Abana and Pharpar, rivers of Damascus, better than all the waters of Israel? May I not wash in them and be clean?" And while asserting that they wait on God for direction, yet argue that *they* should choose the *means.* In the case of Hezekiah there was a *needs be* of the obedience of certain means, simple and near at hand. The clay and spittle used by the Lord Jesus, and gradual restoration of the blind man who believed, the bathing in the pool of Siloam, — all these varied phases of healing and dealing with his people God sets forth for our instruction : and in all these things He saith, " Consider," and " Remember the former things which have been ever of old."

> " Sad heart, cease thy loud complaining,
> Lessons are the children's lot ;
> Songs have ceased, and solace waning,
> But thy Saviour changeth not.
> If thou wilt with Him *abide*,
> Soon thou shalt be satisfied."

Amongst many whose service I have traced on the Continent was one whose hand scattered the first seed of blessing in Italy, before the ban was taken off the gospel, and when the prison awaited the fearless disciple who sighed over the beautiful South, fettered in the bonds of ignorance and priestcraft. And amongst many whom I have recognized appointed to work in the bonds of pain and weakness was a beloved friend of my own, whose patience glorified her Master in the furnace heated seven times beyond its wont. Five incurable diseases for years worked upon a finely strung nervous organization, even before pardon and peace were fully realized. And when the joy of the Lord was her strength, disease deepened and continued with scarcely any amelioration, until the soul of one the dearest to her, who had nursed her through long years, was accorded to her prayers. The fruit of that life of patient suffering who can gather *here?* For my own part, what can I say of my gain by it? Letters from that couch of pain came to me in power and blessing, from one whose face I had

never seen, whose name until then was unknown to me,
bringing me messages of counsel and comfort fresh as
though just breathed by the Holy Spirit, though they
travelled four thousand miles to reach me from the distant land where she tarried, breathing the very air of
heaven. A hidden spring, telling of the source of wisdom and love from whence it sprang, filling the fountain with praise until streams of living water, promised
to those who believe in a living God, refreshed others.
The last effort of her life was the half-finished letter
forwarded to me at her decease, when the pen fell from
her fingers before they stiffened in death, and her last
life work was over for God and for me. And in this
life and the life that is to come her name beams as a
star on my homeward path, and all this and much more
sprang up from " one as good as dead." (Heb. xi. 12.)

In the hospital and many a country infirmary, there
lie for protracted periods some of God's choicest
teachers, who have learned of the Holy Ghost alone,
whose sympathy with suffering and knowledge in the
heavenly science shame some learners, and encourage
others to press on to know Him who is thus communing
with his people. The robust evangelist in his passing
visit would have little ability to impart the confidence
and consolation that a patient sufferer breathes. Many
marvel why their prayers are received for others, and
that for themselves rejected in the way of health and
strength. We cannot always judge of man's position
by the accomplishment of his desires. The wilderness
family aforetime had the desire of their heart (Ps.
lxxviii. 29) ; and often the Lord will show us (if we

wait on Him) that our desire for what is even lawful is not at that time expedient, and the cross that humbles us, and the cup that has embittered all earth's natural pleasures, fenced up the way to the Lord Himself. (Hosea ii. 6.) These are the preparatory seasons for the prosperity of his servants, in which the Lord delighteth; and while all seems bowed down, bruised, and broken, the Lord is saying, "From Me is thy fruit found." (Hosea xiv. 8.) Thus the evening hymn of the soul ascends with the incense, "It is good for me that I have been afflicted." "Oh how great is Thy goodness, which Thou hast laid up for them that fear Thee; which Thou hast wrought for them that trust in Thee before the sons of men!" (Ps. xxxi. 19.) In many of the parables of nature, God teaches us lessons of his dealings, and in all He bids us "consider."

The prickly pear, together with the black bread of the country, form the principal food of the peasants of the southern coasts of Sicily. These gigantic plants, with their golden blossoms and beautiful fruit, enliven with their verdure the otherwise dreary expanse of shore surrounding the city of Catania. The large pale-green leaves, resembling some species of the aloe and common cactus, bear alike the blossom and fruit. Everywhere on the outskirts of the city, on the sandy beach, on acres of lava, where nothing else will grow, this vigorous plant, with its sharp-pointed leaves, lifts up its spears, sometimes forming a formidable fence that neither man nor beast can pass, sometimes in groves that afford shelter from the burning rays of the sun, and everywhere offering its fruit to the traveller, —

a welcome refreshment to those who have learned to handle its thorny mail. When I first examined them, I felt indignant at the wanton mischief (as it appeared to me) that had smitten many of the noblest plants: in some places they had been roughly stricken with a rod or even a heavy staff; in others the leaves were torn asunder, and the juice of the plant, bright as dew-drops, wept from the wounds, and the leaves dropped as if faded and dying.

Months went by, and the sharp tramontane winds were changed for the balmy air and cloudless skies of a Sicilian spring, and I visited the platform of pumice-stone, where the finest specimens I had seen seemed the most cruelly outraged. The wounds had ceased to weep, and the incisions had given richer verdure and life to the plant. Little buds, destined to form the golden blossoms, marked where the strokes had fallen; and· many of the more tender leaves, though nearly severed by the blows, had expanded into a wider sphere, — in fact, had become as it were two leaves on one stem, and brought forth a double proportion of fruit.

· So great is the power of life in these plants that when these vast fields of lava are needed for building ground or for cultivation, orifices are made by dint of pickaxe and hatchet, large enough to admit one of these succulent leaves, with sufficient loam to keep it moist until the root is formed from the strong, thread-like fibres. Then the force in that life is such that it breaks open the rock of lava that defies the hand of man, and works unseen beneath. Thus a leaf breaks the strong rock, and gives its richest fruit where its tears have fallen.

When it has accomplished its labor it is cut down, and houses arise, and vineyards are cultivated, the olive gives forth its oil; and the way for all this fertility springs up from — a wounded leaf that has become a fruit-bearing branch, and broken the strong rock that defied the hand of man.   So everywhere we find the lessons we need laid out for us in the wide book of nature; but like little children, we must follow the hand that points them out, to teach the lessons that they bring us, even as the man among the myrtle-trees. (Zech. i. 10.)   "They that dwell under his shadow shall return; they shall revive as the corn, and grow as the vine: the scent thereof shall be as the wine of Lebanon."   (Hosea xiv. 7.)

CHAPTER V.

WATERS IN THE WILDERNESS.

"In the wilderness shall waters spring out, and rivers in the desert."—Is. xxxv. 6.

WHEN temptation is considered, each individual soul is disposed too frequently to confine it to some special besetment he experiences in his own life and character, and that it is one ; whereas it is so entwined with many that it never stands alone. The form of temptation to each separate soul is so diverse, that like the thorn in the flesh, it is known only to Him who permits it, and who can alone grant the right to discover the enemy's snare, and the grace which is sufficient to sustain, protect, and deliver.

The root of all sin is the sin which doth so easily beset us, — unbelief. This is the parent of all temptation ; this is the fruitful thistle and thorn with which the earth abounds. Still the serpent whispers, " Yea, hath God said ? " still our faithless heart asks, " Is He able ? " and the enemy exalts the pride of intellect against the simplicity of faith, and expediency against the lawful.

But we are not ignorant of his devices. If the finger of God writes his law in our hearts, love will teach us that his commandments are not grievous. "In keeping of them there is great reward." Many little links form a strong chain ; and as the gentle amenities of life, flowing continually to and from a friend we love, rivet the affection and bind one to another, so the love of God, shed abroad in our hearts by the Holy Ghost, will lead us to seek Him as the one object and desire of life. "The upright are his delight," and if we are upright we rely on his power to deliver us from the inborn evil of our own heart, from Satan's insidious attacks, and from the worst of ills, a dead conscience, a rebellious will, and a prayerless heart. (James i. 12.) Perhaps of all the afflictions of God's people, temptation is the most afflictive ; yet it is generally the pioneer of new and unexpected blessings, and closely follows many a sanctified trial. At the baptism of the Lord Jesus, when the voice of the Father declared, " This is my beloved Son, in whom I am well pleased," we read, " then was Jesus led up into the wilderness to be tempted of the devil" ; and from the wilderness He descends in the power of the Spirit to preach, to teach, to call his chosen disciples to follow Him, to heal the sick, and cast out devils. And so that wondrous three-years' ministry began ! The glory God had given Him, He leagued to us : one with Him in service, one with Him in the Father, one with Him in the glory that shall follow, — the eternal weight of glory.

There is no position in which grace should be so fully relied on, or the tender compassion of our risen

Lord more confided in, than the hour of temptation. The power of his resurrection is learned in the fellowship of his sufferings. "For we have not an High-Priest which cannot be touched with the feeling of our infirmities ; but was in all points tempted like as we are, yet without sin. Let us therefore come boldly unto the throne of grace, that we may obtain mercy, and find grace to help in time of need." (Heb. iv. 15, 16.) Wait not until the billows overwhelm you, when Satan by the mysterious power of matter over spirit blindfolds the spiritual vision, and you see only by the senses, you hear what you would not hear, — the voice of the tempter and your own blinded heart as if leagued with Satan ; the watch at the door of the lips no longer set, the nerves agitated, the enemy coming in like a flood, sweeping away every sense of the power and presence of the only Deliverer.

Have you placed yourself in this position, and allowed your feet to be taken in a snare? (for vainly is the snare set in the sight of any bird.) Do you not remember some admonition, some whisper of the Spirit, some word that you recall as the warning that you heeded not, — showing you that the eye of One who never slumbers nor sleeps is ever on you? Perhaps all these heavenly cautions have passed unheeded, and you crossed the threshold of your own will. "Hast thou not procured this unto thyself, in that thou hast forsaken the Lord thy God, when He led thee by the way?" And now you know not how to return. "The Lord of hosts is the God of Israel, even a God to Israel!" (1 Chron. xvii. 24.) Cry to Him just where you are, "Thou who performest all things for me, hear and save!" For has He not said unto thee, "I am thy salvation?" cry to Him!

"How cry when the very sense of his presence is gone, and unbelief is eating into my soul? I am as one cast out of sight."

I tell you nay. He hears your sob, your sigh, your groan, and counts each one as a prayer. The very desire to return to the Rock of your heart, though you realize it not, is a messenger of the God of all consolation, and comes from Himself: for the dove finds no rest for the sole of her foot until the ark is her refuge; the cords of love that bind you so sharply are to draw you where He would have you. Only trust Him, and soon you will say with David, " In my distress I called upon the Lord, and cried to *my* God: and He did hear my voice out of his temple, and my cry did enter into his ears." The sorrowful wanderer, with the shadows deepening around him, believes God afar off. Nay, He is near, very near. Glorify Him just where you are, by *believing in his love.* In the shadows of Satanic power upon the soul, God, as seen in the face of Jesus Christ, is in measure obliterated, and is the God from whom we would fain hide ourselves. We see ourselves as we are, and we are afraid of Him; for the God presented to the terrified heart by the enemy is a God of wrath and vengeance, and not *our* God.

The heart is never so little on the watch as after some protracted suffering, or deliverance from some expected woe. The mind has been softened and the flesh subdued by suspense and sorrow, and in the grateful or joyous emotion that pervades the soul, he

believes that this particular sin is destroyed ; or perhaps
he falls into a deeper snare, and imagines that the root
of sin is destroyed altogether, — forgetting that it has
poisoned the source of our natural life, and that there
is no action, no offering of even our holy things, which
does not need his sacrifice of the great High-Priest.
Union with Christ does not imply that temptation is
over, and conflict is at an end. Far otherwise : it is
only then that we are in a position to resist the devil,
mortify our members which are upon the earth, fight
the good fight of faith, wrestle against wicked spirits
in heavenly places, and in Him overcome. All this
implies power, in abiding in the only source of power,
to attain — what? A knowledge of *Him*, the power of
his resurrection, and the fellowship of his sufferings
being made conformable to his death. " If we say that
we have no sin, we deceive ourselves, and the truth is
not in us. If we confess our sins, He is faithful and
just to forgive us our sins, and to cleanse us from all
unrighteousness." (1 John i. 8, 9.) We hear often of
the sinless state of perfection that charms the ear and
delights the heart of many an earnest child of the Kingdom. This is what he longs for, desires after ; but let
him remember that He who can keep him from falling
does not forsake him ; that He has fallen to him, and is our
Advocate with the Father, even Jesus Christ the Righteous. Let us give thanks at " the remembrance of his
holiness." In the flesh dwelleth no good thing ; and if
we ignore this, and suppose from the intensity of our
joy, and the absence of our usual points of attack, that
we have at last something in which we may triumph,

He who reads the heart may open to us the field of battle which lies unseen around us, to mortify our members which are on the earth. If Satan has left us for a season, we have yet a world-wide battle-field; so that we shall cry, " Who can understand his errors? cleanse thou me from secret faults. Keep back thy servant also from presumptuous sins ; let them not have dominion over me." Satan has *considered* you from your cradle to this day, and he chooses the time, season, and opportunity for setting the snare which shall be best suited to entrap you. Your safety is in the Rock. Turn ye to the Stronghold. We cannot set forth joy as the seal of communion, neither as the *object* of communion, — as if there can be no abiding unless joy preponderates, to the discouragement of timid believers who, though not joyful, are faithful followers of the Lamb. His joy is fulfilled in our abiding in Him, and the peace that passeth all understanding lies in the depth of the deep well. Joy sparkles on its surface ; clouds may obscure it, but cannot reach the source. We cannot claim joy as an attainment. Rejoice in the *Lord* always, and again I say, rejoice. We do not *attain* to it : it belongs to the veriest babe in Christ as to the veteran soldier, and " joy in the God of my salvation " remains ; and though obscured, let any touch the dumb chord, and it will answer to that one name above all names. We know the music is only sleeping. Rejoice in the *Lord*, " wherein ye *greatly* rejoice, though now for a season (if need be) ye are in heaviness through manifold temptations : that the trial of your faith, being much more precious than of gold that perisheth, though it be tried with fire." (1 Peter i. 6, 7.)

A Christian lady, more extensively used of the Lord than almost any one I have known, was occasionally bowed down in an outwardly joyless state, which I have since believed was used greatly to the prosperity of her soul, by humbling her and keeping alive her sympathies for others ; but she seemed for brief seasons as if shut out from the light of heaven, though naturally one of the most joyful of women. She knew my love and sympathy with her, and travelled many miles to tell me her sorrow, her disappointment in herself.

" But you love the Lord still, do you not? He is the same yesterday, to-day, and forever," I inquired after listening to her sorrows, while her pale, sad face attested their reality.

" Love Him? O my dear, yes," she exclaimed with sudden animation. " I told Him this morning, that if I did not love Him, I could truly say I do not love anything or any one else" ; and as her heart (which she called deserted) looked on to what He had done for her and what He had been to her, instead of what she had done and what she had been to Him, she took up the strain, " He loved me, and gave Himself for me," and broke down in happy tears of praise. She was called to visit one darker 'neath the cloud and deeper 'neath the flood of great waters than herself. She listened to a tale of woe more sad than her own ; and " You love the Lord," said my friend, " but because of this sin you say the Lord can no longer love you. 'Jesus Christ came into the world to save sinners, of whom I am the chief,' but he does not love you : is that it?" " Yes,

yes," replied the broken-hearted woman, " that is it; but all his judgments are right, and if He casts me into hell. I will spend eternity in singing 'Praise the Lord.'" "Nay," said my friend with her own bright smile, "that can never be : such songs would not be allowed in hell; they would turn you out." The snare was broken, and she was delivered. " A word in season, how good it is !" with the sympathy of one who has passed that way before. "Trust in Him at *all times;* ye people, pour out your heart before Him : God is a refuge for us."

Do not be disheartened because your present temptation is a strange thing. The Lord knows that you have not passed this way heretofore. But fear not! He is not changed. Dwell on the promises He has given for your comfort, the promise that He will never leave nor forsake ; He knoweth that we are dust. There are a thousand counsels to keep us from falling, and as many to raise and restore you. Look back on his many deliverances by ways and means man could never have devised or executed, and be persuaded to trust Him fully. He strove mightily in you aforetime, and did wondrously for you, and left you conqueror ; and you can cry, "Save me from the lion's mouth : for Thou hast heard me from the horns of the unicorns." (Ps. xxii. 21.) Or if the remembrance of a former defeat arises, let it be a warning, and the incentive for vigilance to-day. Strength is born of the strong ; for your weakness and natural cowardice, there stands prepared the power of the endless life in Him who is made unto us " wisdom, and righteousness, and sanctification, and redemption." Therefore be strong in the Lord, and in the power of his might. They that know Thy name shall put their trust in Thee, for thou, Lord, hast not forsaken them that seek Thee "; and what is his name? The *faithful and true!* The Bible has become a dead letter, prayer seems stilled, service a labor, the light of life as it were extinguished. Does it please the Lord that you should be thus? Read on: you know not when the Spirit may move on the troubled waters, and you shall be healed; pray, though the utterance is broken and cold; believe in his love, though the sorrows of death compass you, though all seems desolate; seek his face still, wait for Him. It is confidencei n the love and faithfulness and power of the Lord that He honors. Succumbing to one temptation has brought others, and now you are tempted to disbelieve his promises, and dishonor Him by doubt of his love. Look away from yourself and your deservings, — to Himself. "Once," said a dear young Christian to me, — "once I thought I could *run* in the ways of the Lord; but now I find I cannot walk or stand!" If the child feels too strong to need the right hand of a faithful God to lead him, it is love that allows him to stumble and fall, to teach him, "Without Me ye can do nothing." When Gideon was weak, he fought the Lord's battles, and would be assured of every step he took in the fear of the Lord; but when Gideon was strong he made an idol, and caused others to go astray after a false god. David, after his many deliverances and triumphs in the time of prosperity, becomes covetous of another man's wife, and falls. (2 Sam. vii. 9.) Hezekiah, who trusted in the Lord. and clave to Him (2 Kings xviii. 5, 6), becomes vainglorious in the time of health and peace. When the world speaks flattering words of the child of God, then is the need-be of the cry, " Woe, woe, and beware," for every one that doeth evil hateth the light. Peter, who had seen the glory on Mount Tabor, and many a time had shared the hours of privacy with his Divine Master in the garden, deserts Him at the cross, and denies Him in the judgment hall. The opinion of a servant-maid seems a contemptible snare, but something meaner than the approval of the Hebrew damsel has been used to draw our careless steps astray. The fall of Peter contrasts with the sin of Judas. When the high-priest covenanted with Judas to betray the Lord of glory for thirty pieces of silver, Judas *sought* opportunity to betray him. There was no fall with the false disciple : he was always in the position of sin, and ready to commit the evil deed. Covetousness was already working when the broken alabaster box created his displeasure, fostered daily by his depredations out of the bag he bore ; for he was a thief. The true disciple wept bitterly, and the Lord looked on him, and restored him, and sent him forth to feed his people, stronger that he had learned his own weakness and his Master's faithful love. The traitor did not seek the Holy One he had betrayed with a kiss : he went forth and hung himself.

Jonah flies from the service of God, but he cannot fly from God, who follows him in chastening and blessing. Elijah, who stands before us as the fearless prophet, fails before a wicked woman's threat and flies into the desert; but the Lord he had hitherto faithfully served, deals with him in tenderness, and honors him beyond all other prophets since the days of Enoch. He fled to the wilderness, but a faithful God was there! Twice he must partake of heaven-sent food and sleep must restore the sad-hearted man before he could pursue his journey, — a journey that had a purpose in it, even to bring him face to face with the Lord at Horeb. The Lord *might* have put him to shame before his enemies, or left him the victim of his unbelieving fears; but He deals with the weary man as a *Father*, not as a Judge, and brings him alone with Himself.

Oh, to honor God by believing that we are dear to Him, surely as dear as his people of old, "Thou answeredst them, O Lord our God: Thou wast a God that forgavest *them*, though Thou tookest vengeance of their inventions"! And how much more hath He done for you, what more *can* He do? Temptation and trial are still the discipline of the wilderness family: not one halt in that desert march could have been spared, not one could have been shortened; as to *them* he says unto you, "Thou calledst in trouble, and I delivered *thee;* I answered thee in the secret place of thunder: I proved thee at the waters of Meribah."

THE PRISONER OF THE LORD.

BY ANNA SHIPTON.

"The Lord openeth the eyes of the blind: the Lord raiseth them that are bowed down." — PSALM cxlvi. 8.

"O my dove, that art in the clefts of the rock, in the secret places of the stairs, let me see thy countenance, let me hear thy voice; for sweet is thy voice, and thy countenance is comely." — SONG OF SOLOMON ii. 14.

"Many are reaping the harvest fields,
And I lie here alone,
Counting the time by the dreary night:
Oh, when will the day be gone?

"Some lead the flock to the mountain height,
And some to the dewy lawn;
And the fishers their nets from the silvery tide,
The weight of their spoil have drawn:

"But I lie here with my yearning heart
On labor I long to share;
My lattice is dark, and heavy my chain,
And fetters I still must wear."

The plaint had ceased from the maiden's lips,
When over the mountains spread
A ray more bright than the morning star;
It gleamed on a scroll *unread.*

A scroll that told of a Father's love,
Of his might, his way, and his will;
Of the faithful Friend who never forsakes,
The Master who loves her still.

Light fell on her tears on her cheek so wan,
And now on her garments white,
As she watched the stars as they rose and set
In the shade of the deepening night.

A darker gloom had shadowed her brow
    Than ever was there before,
When a cry arose, "The Master is come!
    He stands at the bolted door."

Oh, gentle the voice of that midnight Guest,
    And tender the Friend that came
To open her lattice and tune her harp,
    And call his child by her name.

"Yea, some are afar on the waters wide,
    And some on the mountain height;
But couldst thou not watch one hour with Me,
    In the shade of the silent night?

"I came with the cloud that covered thy earth,
    And thy lips have ceased to sing;
I sent the mist on thy brain, and quelled
    Thy fair imagining.

"O Child of my love! thy chain I wrought,
    And soon shalt thou lay it by;
In my Father's house thou shalt bless the day
    Of thy brief captivity.

"Thy brethren toil in fields afar,
    And long for thy harp's sweet tone;
But, hidden within my sanctuary,
    Thy service hath well been done.

"My wanderers rest 'neath the sea-girt rock
    To list to the minstrel's strain,
And hearts bowed down by their earthly toil
    Take courage, and hope again.

"But . . . give me thy harp — 't is all unstrung;
    Go forth to thy chosen lot:
The Master has need of his prison bird,
    But the prisoner heeds Him not!

" Choose now what seemeth the better part,
  And glad may thy service be ;
But never so dear in the sunny noon
  As thy midnight song to me."

The fetters fell from the maiden's hands
  As the midnight Guest drew nigh ;
The threshold is past, — she standeth free,
  In the joy of liberty !

One moment she gazed on the wounded Hand
  That opened the bolted door ;
Then back she turned to her starlit cell,
  And the chain she weeping wore.

The prison was changed to a banquet hall,
  (And the banner that waved was "Love ") ;
'T was paved with the mercies of bygone years,
  Ere her foolish heart could rove.

Like diamonds sparkled her fetters then,
  As silk was her iron chain ;
She kissed each link with its chiselled gem,
  And welcomed them back again.

" How sweet is the bondage ! " the maiden cried,
  To the fetters of old restored ;
" I am not alone in my midnight watch :
  My Keeper is Christ my Lord ! "

Her harp is tuned by the Master's hand,
  For his prisoner's songs below ;
And sweeter the lesson of Jesus' love
  Than ever the freed can know.

The north wind and the south wind (Sol. Song iv. 16)
must blow upon the garden of the Lord, and we shall
testify that the tempest we thought would destroy us

only worked the will of Him who aforetimes caused the waters to stand as a heap to make Himself a glorious name. When the rough wind sweeps over the garden, we cannot enjoy the fragrance of the flowers; but it is preparing the plants for greater fruitfulness. The storm that seemed sent to uproot them only carried away dry leaves and dead branches of the year that has gone, and the faded blossoms swept from the boughs have left fruit behind. "Fury is not in Me: who would set the briers and thorns against Me in battle? I would go through them, I would burn them together. Or let him take hold of my strength, that he may make peace with Me, and he shall make peace with Me." (Is. xxvii. 4, 5.) No matter if our temptation be as Gideon's or David's or Solomon's or Hezekiah's or Elijah's or Peter's, it will always seem a "strange" thing until the Holy Spirit opens the eyes to see the Lord.

The child who has wandered from his father's house is still his father's child. Jehoshaphat, though snared into becoming one with the ungodly, is not deserted, and stands forth as one of the examples for our learning of the faithfulness of God. It is said that Ahab *persuaded* him to go with him. The steps of declension are insidious, whether it be in gross sin, or standing in the way of sinners, which often leads to it. Jehoshaphat (translated, "whom the Lord judges," — better to be judged by the Lord than condemned with the world) goes down to the king of Israel; and Ahab made a feast in his honor, and Jehoshaphat became the guest of the man who was "the enemy of God," without any aim but to receive honor of man. " The friendship of the world is enmity with God. Whosoever therefore will be a friend of the world is the enemy of God." (James iv. 4.) He was not called there in the Lord's service, nor do we read that there was any blessing attending his presence ; for even the true prophet who warned the king was not believed by the ally of the king. By the mercy of God he returns in peace ; but the Lord does not leave him without reproof, and sends his prophet to rebuke him. (2 Chron. xix. 2.) If the child of God meddles with that to which he is not called, — maybe from idle leisure, or natural activity, or what is inaptly termed "good nature," — he will generally find it is a snare to entice him out of the position of service or testimony in which the Lord has placed him. The false king whom Jehoshaphat was so ready to help, persuades him to disguise himself in the robes of God's enemies, so that the armies did not know one king from another ; but the Lord knows his own in whatsoever motley garb they be arrayed, and the cry of his child, ready to perish, reaches *his* ear who had protected him, and put the fear of him on the nations round about. His influence extended over many kingdoms ; and thus Ahab, Jehoram, and Ahaziah were led to seek him, not because the God of Israel was his defence and was *his* God, but because they expected some temporal benefit to be derived from the association. Kings sent presents to him, the Philistines brought a tribute of silver, the Arabians flocks of sheep and cattle. He had " honor and riches in abundance," but it did not prevent him

from desiring more.   He joins affinity with the son of
Ahab, and thus sprang the family alliance ; for his son
took the daughter of Ahab to wife, and he walked not
after his father, but after the evil ways of the house of
Ahab.

Jehoram persuades Jehoshaphat, as Ahab his father
had done, to go up to battle with him against Moab,
the enemy of Israel.   How far Jehoshaphat was permitted to stand in the counsel of the ungodly for the
destruction of Moab, and the witness of the Lord's
protection and deliverance to his own people, we know
not.   He alone seeth the heart, and judges not according to the sight of our eyes.   But we see that for the
sake of the child of God, though out of the way, there
falls a blessing ; and the ditches dug in obedience to
the Lord were filled with water for the thirsty host and
exhausted cattle and horses.   For his sake only the
prophet who stands before the Lord brings the word of
the Lord ; for his sake the water flows without any natural means, so that none could declare a sudden storm
had filled the valley with water ; for his sake the meat
offering was offered, and faith in that offering caused
the promised streams to flow in the channels prepared
to receive it ; for his sake the great army of Moab fled
before the army of Israel, and that which gave refreshment to the fainting host was used to the discomfiture
of their enemies.   " Blessed is the man whose strength
is in Thee ; in whose heart are the ways of them, who
passing through the valley of Baca make it a well ; the
rain also filleth the pools.   They go from strength to
strength, every one of them in Zion appeareth before

God." (Ps. lxxxiv. 5, 6, 7.) And so it shall ever be : the ditches in the valley that our feeble hands have made at his command shall be filled with living water from the fountain of Israel, by ways that man knows not.

Jehoshaphat had " riches in abundance " ; and moreover, in the memorable battle in which the Lord fought for him against Ammon, Moab, and Mount Seir, the spoil of precious jewels and treasures was so great that after three days' gathering of it, it was more than they could carry away : yet he desired more. For this purpose he joined Ahaziah of the house of Ahab in building ships at Eziongaber, to go to Ophir for more gold. But the ships were broken, so that he could not accomplish his purpose, and was thus preserved from such close intercourse with his ungodly ally, " a king who did very wickedly," and thus was saved from the temptation of amassing further wealth. If the Lord in mercy breaks the vessels that we have builded to sail after the imaginations of our own foolish heart, let us take note of his mercy and not build them again. It is very helpful to consider the Lord's dealings with ourselves and with those of others whose lives are manifested to us by the Spirit, and to read his faithfulness in chastening and rebuke, both in the case of the broken ships and the alliance with Ahab. As he returned from the battle where his cry to God had saved him, the prophet met him, and denounced the wrath of God on him for " loving them that hate the Lord." How that anger was expressed we know not, but Jehoshaphat knew ; and we know, though all seem prosperity and peace to others, that if we have joined affinity with Ahab's race, or the thing which we have done " displeased the Lord," the light of our life is obscured, and we walk as blind men. " The thing that *David did displeased the Lord.*" Therewith we read the chastening. The soul taught of God feels his displeasure and knows the chastening hand, though it is not always seen by man, but recognized by the wilful child and disobedient servant when alone before God. (Heb. xii. 6, 7.)

Let us be aware of the Enemy when tempted to distrust God's unchanging love. When tempted to suspect the absent one, whose love until now we have never doubted, we recall the past. Perhaps we turn to the written words that breathed the affection once so precious to us ; we remember the years of faithful tenderness ; and thoughts of the frank glance and tone of one who has never dissimulated dispels the suspicion that Satan seeks to call forth in the heart, to tempt and harass it. If we listen to the Tempter we may believe our love misplaced, and ask sadly, " Am I deceived after all ; can all have changed ! "

Yes, we know that all *can* change but God, who alone can say, " I will never fail thee nor forsake thee." In Him is no shadow of turning ; He has said, " I am the Lord, I change not ! " Let us go back to his written words, to his love that sought us and saved us, to the mercies every day new, to the grace that has restored us from falls only He could discern, and deliverances from temptation only his pitiful eye looked upon. As He was, so is He to-day ; for God is an eternal " I Am," a very present God, an unchangeable Friend, He has said it ; He has given to us his Son " Jesus Christ, the same yesterday, to-day, and forever," and " in Him dwelleth all the fulness of the Godhead bodily." (Col. ii. 9.)

Nothing can satisfy the renewed soul but eternal realities ; and there is no more amazing reality than that " God so loved the world that He gave his only begotten Son, that whosoever believed on Him should not perish, but have everlasting life," and that He against whom we have so often offended pardons our transgressions, and remembers our iniquities no more ! Could the bride delighting in the love of the lover of her youth be tempted by evil men to the haunts of vice? would she not turn away in horror and dismay at the invitation to betray, by her own dishonor, the honor of him she loves? Only believe in that stupendous Love that rests on *you* just as you are, who deals with you in love that you may be such as He would have you. " This is the victory that overcometh the world, even our faith." Personal dealing with the living, loving Lord, faithful to chasten, faithful to restore, shall keep the heart in the love of Christ which passeth knowledge. Teach it, preach it, live on it and in it, and there shall spring forth such abundant seed from one though " as good as dead, so many as the stars of the sky in multitude, and as the sand which is by the sea-shore innumerable " (Heb. xi. 12.)

The Serpent, who was declared more subtle than any beast of the field, is more subtle still. To-day, as in Eden, he will seek to prove your God a liar ! Nay : what God hath promised, that will He do ; and what He hath declared himself in your behalf, that will He be! "I the Lord have spoken it, and will do it." (Ez. xxii. 14.)

The hidden enemies of the Lord, that may have lain unconsciously hidden in the heart, will arise and rebel when least looked for. Then the soul will exclaim like Jacob, "All these things are against me!" Nay: God is working for your enlargement and preparing the way for that which you have long ago been so urgent for Him to grant, — a deeper knowledge of Himself. The battles of the Lord are not fought alike: some victories are gained by the meanest instrumentality, like lamps and broken pitchers; some aggressively, as David's (1 Chron. xiv.); some as Hezekiah's, where the angel of destruction slays the enemy; and others as Jehoshaphat's, in the power of prayer and praise, when the man of faith is commanded to stand still and see the salvation of God, believing in his truth and praising for a victory as yet unseen. To the observant soul who desires a knowledge of the will and power of the Lord, the Holy Spirit has many modes of action, and various ways of communicating light and strength; He does not use the same means at all times, neither in the same season. We must not copy others in regard to God's individual teaching. The word of God, with its precepts and teaching, lies open to every upright soul who seeks safety, deliverance from his enemies. It is not your care to order the battle; follow the Conqueror, "casting all your care upon Him, for he careth for you."

"I the Lord have spoken and have done it." (Ez. xvii. 24.) Believe only: believe in the love which has called and chosen thee, upheld and delivered thee, washed thee and healed thee, instructed and led thee, guided and chastened thee. Believe in his everlasting, unchangeable love, and the loving-kindness which drew thee to Him ; and thou, though the feeblest of his servants, the most timid and faltering of his children, shall become day by day a defenced city, an iron pillar, a brazen wall, and they shall fight against thee and shall not prevail against thee, for the Lord is with thee to deliver thee. Day by day we need to set before us to uphold us in the hour of temptation, to keep us from it and to raise us if fallen, is to believe in the love and faithfulness of God in his word and his dealings.

Bear with me while I tell you of the faith in a father's love that taughtme a lesson ; would that I had earlier learned to profit by it !

" The love of little Dolly for her father, and the father's love to his first-born, were the very life of the child's heart, ruling her actions and giving the spring to her joys, so that it shadowed forth to many a reflective mind the power of abiding in divine love. But the day came when Dolly was no longer the sole object of consideration in her father's house. ' A man-child was born unto him, making him very glad.' A brother now must share the love hitherto exclusively bestowed on herself. The nurse brought the infant to his father, who took it in his arms and walked the room with undisguised thankfulness for his new treasure ; nor did he observe that he was not alone until a low, quivering sob from a distant part of the room attracted his attention. With her face hidden in her hands and her head bent to her knees, the young soul was learning its first lesson in life. Her grief was so profound that her father strove in vain to win her from the shadowed corner in which she had taken refuge. But when he approached her, her bursting heart could no longer withstand the voice of tender persuasion as to the cause of her grief; and between the sobs that rent her heart was heard the desolate cry, 'Father does not love his Dolly any more!'''

Her father read the secret of the young heart's anguish, and sending for the nurse to take the infant, they two were left alone. Then he folded his little one in his arms, and pressed her silently to his breast, in full comprehension of sympathy; beneath the influence of that mute caress, the heaving chest was still, the tears ceased to flow. He bade her look into his face. The dark eyes, still glittering with tears, gazed steadfastly into the loving face of one who had never deceived her : her father, her teacher, her dear familiar companion, her friend! Slowly and impressively he said, " Now, Dolly, believe father : he loves his Dolly; he will *always* love his Dolly, always." The child looked, listened, and *believed;* her tears were dried, her smiles returned ; and the love of her heart, crushed by outward temptation, sprang up again from that assurance. Why? *Because she believed.* That night the father bent over his child as she slept : the lisping lips of the little sleeper murmured again and again in slumber the sweet content, the secret of her peace, — " Father loves his Dolly ; he will always love his Dolly, always, always." O feeble, doubting heart, let this

little child teach *thee!* (2 Cor. iv. 6, 7.) Take
ye also of the best wine, " that goeth down sweetly,
causing the lips of those that are asleep to speak."
(Sol. Song vii. 9.) Oh, better than father and mother,
so God loveth *thee* with a love that knoweth no dimi-
nution ; and though thy cold heart suspects his love
when all things seem against thee, He loves thee still.
He has written, " I am the Lord, I change not." Hast
thou looked to Him in the face of Jesus Christ? Hast
thou listened? *Hast thou believed?* (Is. xxvi. 3.) The
consideration of the kindness of the Lord, who knoweth
how to deliver the good out of temptation, and his
mercy to the fallen, will never lead to licentiousness.
We need to be strengthened and to strengthen others
against the Tempter, let him come in whatsoever guise
he may ; but also we need to be reminded of that faithful Friend who has so often made the way of escape
before it was too late, or if He has left us to try our
heart (2 Chron. xxxii. 31), to still cleave to the
remembrance of the Merciful High Priest. It has
fallen to me to be brought in contact, in late days, with
despairing souls. Some have sought a perfection that
was never found out of the all-perfect sinless Son of
God ; and others have never learned that only as
they abide in Him can they dwell in the peace which
his presence alone gives, and while seeking to walk
according to his law, have not known that a *personal*
trust in a crucified and risen Saviour is the sole
power of the believer's walk. Satan loves to eject
hard thoughts against the Lord God, merciful and
gracious, long-suffering, and abundant in goodness and

truth. Yet the Lord has declared Himself "easy to be entreated." Some have declared that they have sinned past hope ; and the promise of their life blighted, they have sunk into hopeless misery. In every case, they *have not believed* in the eternal *love of God* to his child. "Those loved thee with an everlasting love." It is not to be supposed that any soul of a believer falls into sin without some remonstrance of the Holy Spirit. "Be not high-minded, but fear." We know not when we may be led by some device of the devil, to join affinity with those who will lead us astray, and we say to them, "We are as thou art, and our people as your people"; how we may be led to spend our labor for that which is not bread, and our strength for that which satisfieth not; how David's sin and Solomon's snares may cause us to stumble, though now we say in terror, "Though all should forsake Thee, yet will not I." "Is thy servant a dog that he should do this thing?" There are no apologies for sin. The child of God makes none and seeks none. Unbelief is the parent of all transgression from Adam unto this day. Nay: it is to the love and faithfulness of God to which I will point, to the tempted and to the fallen ! His faithfulness and his tenderness can alone melt the frozen sluices of broken hearts, and make them beat sweet music. Yes! these are the triumphs in heavenly places, on which principalities and powers of the world to come look and wonder ! "A troop may overcome him, but he shall overcome at the last." The battle in the heart, on which God alone looks down, wins fairer crowns than any know but the Conqueror.

" Be not afraid nor dismayed ; the battle is not yours, but God's." If for the covenant God made with David, He showed mercy to the *house* of David, how much more will he show mercy for the sake of David's Lord! And He *has* covenanted with his own forever, never to leave, — never, never to forsake them. The poison of sin is from the Serpent's sting, and only the power of the Heavenly Physician can purge the conscience from dead works, and cleanse the putrid sores. Mysterious as are these afflictions of temptation, let us not despair. The Lord can carry on his wondrous work unseen and unjudged by man.

Men are appalled by the effects of seduction of the gambling-table ; but only the gambler knows the fascination that leads on step by step to ruin. From the loss and gain of an inconsiderable sum, he at last in despair takes his life, because he dares no longer look on the past. In the environs of Nice, more frightful tragedies are enacted than ever reach the sickening ear of the strangers dwelling on the lovely shores of the Riviera. Some travellers cross the threshold of Circe's den, to " study life," as they tell you ; and it ends in death — on which they have never meditated. Not long since, two young orphan girls of good family and large fortune, tempted by the beauty of the place, the surrounding gardens, and the fine climate, took up their residence in Monaco, where is spread lavishly abroad all that can charm the eye and enervate the mind. Like many other visitors, they were drawn by curiosity to the gaming-table, to watch the poor victims that surrounded it, — to mark the hope and fear, elation and despair, exhibited in the countenances of the players; it was more real and more exciting than the theatre or a sensational novel. Tempted to make the experiment for themselves, they staked a trifling sum, and gained. Again they played, — and lost. They had known the hope and fear; but now, excited by the poisonous fascination, they returned again in hope of retrieving their loss. They staked larger sums, and yet larger, until they were penniless. They were strangers; there were none to say, " Come away, there is hope; life is still yours." Their great personal attractions led the birds of prey to desire to retain them to lure others to destruction. But the young hearts loathed the shameless proposal. So hand in hand they flung themselves into the sea, whose fair shores had won them to seek that place where Satan's seat is, and where his servants watch for the souls of the unwary. Yet, mournful as is this picture, it is less terrible than many continually set before the eye in the soul-destroying atmosphere of Monaco. It is a type of the world's wide gambling-table, but its results are not always seen in the lives of those who step by step take *all*, and lose peace, life, and immortality. If we join affinity with the world, we soon fall into pleasing man, and are ready to say, " I am as thou art, and my people as thy people "; and if our ships are not broken and our idols burned with fire, and all our pleasant places in the wilderness laid waste, so that we cannot attain the unlawful gain we covet, we shall fall by almost imperceptible degrees into the darkness of those who never rejoiced in the light, or knew what it is to believe in the Holy Ghost, communion of saints, forgiveness of sins, and the life everlasting. Let us count among our remembered mercies our withered gourds, our broken ships, which show forth the love and faithfulness of God; for to dwell in the continual realization of his love and faithfulness will be to enliven our own. Who does not remember the day when, conscious of wandering feet, we have paused, expecting judgment, — and lo, a blessing as unlooked-for as undeserved has suddenly fallen, so that our hearts, broken by the love that forgave, melted like the silver in the smelting pot beneath the warmth of a Father's forgiveness? So He restoreth my soul! How? not in bodily activity, but in patient waiting and believing on his word. "I will not cast out." The promise is to those who faint by reason of their weakness, that by *waiting* they shall soar into the conscious rest of a Crucified and Risen Lord. "Then shall they run and not be weary, and they shall walk and not faint."

CHAPTER VI.

RIVERS AMONG THE ROCKS.

"AN two walk together except they be agreed?" To walk with God we need the obedience of faith, the recollection of the Lord's way with us in the past, the consideration of his word and testimony, and that fellowships in the Holy Ghost which shall reveal his will, witness to our spirits, reprove, strengthen, and encourage us in the life of faith.

To walk with God is a life far removed from superstition or carnal imagination. It is the simple act of faith that keeps us in the realized presence of Him with whom we desire to walk.

The angel of the covenant under the law (Ex. xxiii. 20, 21, 22) and the risen Lord and Saviour (Matt. xxviii. 18, 19, 20 ; Heb. x. 16, 17) present to us the aspects of the two dispensations. The smitten rock of the wilderness has fulfilled the righteousness of God ; and only as we abide *in* Him do we become partakers of that righteousness, and are enabled to walk with Him.

If all the wild vagaries of imagination were to be received as the action of the Spirit of God, we should soon be in the position of the spiritists, and become the sport and prey of the Evil One; and if we accepted every impulse of the natural mind as the guidance of the Holy Spirit, we should fall into temptation of the direst kind. On one side we may neglect to seek counsel of the Lord in matters which seem unimportant, and on the other hand wait for some visible token when our duty lies before us; thus we should become entangled in the Enemy's snare of waiting for manifestations. To walk with God in the happy freedom of a little child is far removed from bondage, which term I have heard more than once applied to a state of perpetual dependence on Him.

A young man from a large store called to see me. He was a Christian, away from all Christian fellowship and instruction. The lines of care and anxiety on his pale face gave him at first sight the appearance of an old man. He told me he was greatly perplexed in regard to the Holy Spirit's work within. He was desirous to walk with God, to please Him, but he did not know how, and his anxiety was often so great that his occupation was a continual burden to him. He dared scarcely make up a parcel of goods or write an invoice, without fearing that it had not been done in a manner that would please the Lord. In every act of his life he served the Lord as a bondsman, and not as an obedient child redeemed and beloved in the Beloved. Instead of reading his Bible and pondering its precepts, and believing in the love of God fully set forth for the most timid soul, he was always looking for special signs, which he could interpret to mean that the Lord was satisfied with him. He had not observed the word, " Whatsoever ye do, do it heartily, as to the *Lord*, and not unto men " ; and whatsoever is done heartily to the Lord will stand.

It was no difficult task to set before this sorrowful but truly earnest spirit that it was the lack of " casting all " his care upon the One who careth for him that kept him mourning all his days, and dishonored the gracious Lord who had called him to testify of His sufficiency. Having punctually made up his parcel and carefully written his invoice, *he pleased the Lord;* for he thus fulfilled his duty to his employer, whom he had engaged to serve for a certain salary, and *his* honesty and fidelity for his earthly master could only be sustained by the power of his Master in heaven. It was my joy to see him released.

" Looking unto Jesus," in faithful, persevering application to the service to which he calls, is true faith. It does not consist in spasmodic efforts after the marvellous, or in a life of languid ease that does not seek God in circumstances, and therefore cannot know Him, save as a God afar off or a Father unreconciled. The joy and peace of committing everything to the Lord is the strength of the believer's walk, for He has declared, "Without *Me* ye can do nothing." But this must not be received in the spirit of fear, but in the assurance that whatsoever has been done according to his commandment and committed to Him is accepted for Jesus' sake.

In patient waiting, and in continual meditation in the Word, many a warning is given for our daily walk, the reproof administered, the counsel set forth, for the very perplexity that distresses us. The lives of those whom God has chosen to stand before Him are vocal to the listening soul. The patriarchs and prophets and apostles, the great cloud of witnesses, all lived for our instruction, and He who came to do his Father's will perfectly, speaks as aforetime to the soul that seeks Him.

The precepts for walking with God are contained in his word, but the Holy Spirit must reveal them unto us, according to our present necessity ; for He has promised to satisfy all our need, according to his riches in glory by Christ Jesus. He has *promised* to instruct and teach us in the way we shall go (Ps. xxxii. 8) ; that we shall recognize his voice saying, " *This* is the way ; walk ye in it," and by faith and patience we shall inherit the promises.

There are seasons when we receive light on our path immediately that we have asked for it, either within or direction in our service, or counsel in our difficulties. But be not tempted to doubt because the answer tarries, that therefore your prayer for light, guidance, and instruction is unheeded. Faith must lead you up this mountain. (1 Kings xviii. 43.) You may have to look seven times before the little cloud like a man's hand rises as the precursor of the coming rain.

This age is specially the age of external progress, of things brought to the evidence of the eye and the touch by carnal reasoning ; and there is great danger, even among the children of the Kingdom, of walking and wanting to walk by sense, and not by faith. If you have sought Him, — for faith is needed to climb the mountain seven times as once. — believe that He hears and answers, even if you do not see the result; for has He not written, "I will bring the blind by a way that they knew not; I will lead them in paths that they have not known: I will make darkness light before them, and crooked things straight. These things will I do unto them, and not forsake them"? (Isa. xiii. 16.)

If we walk with God we shall not form our own plan of service, for oftentimes He sends us forth to do that for which we feel very little inclined; but He can prepare us for everything He needs, and when He gives the power, it often sets at naught our natural acquirements. Some laborers, valuable in their sphere, become useless if removed from it; but the emptying from vessel to vessel is needed for the purifying of the wine. There is no true service unless our own soul has first fed upon that which He presents to others, no matter whether it be conversation with a class of Sunday scholars or an address from the platform. The word of God is so rich that after the children are sufficed, seven baskets full will remain of the bread the Lord has broken to his disciple, to distribute to those outside after the disciple himself has been nourished. We must not suppose that we are rejected because He calls us to another employment than formerly, or even lays us down to *wait* his will and watch his way and learn of *Him.* If the Lord has called us where we are, He will give us all that is needed to fulfil that position, if we are looking to *Him* and willing to do his will, instead of striving after the service from which it has pleased Him to withdraw us.

If the master of the house sends his gardener with a letter to a friend, which he needs faithfully delivered, and he is more attached to his master than to his work, he should be as ready to carry his letter as to gather his figs and prune his vine. The interruption of work against our will may sometimes be an obstacle of Satan to prevent its accomplishment, or it may be permitted as the trial of patience ; but if we commit the obstacle to the Lord, be assured that He will not allow his dear servant to suffer loss when his glory has been that servant's aim. He has said, " I will help thee, I will guide thee with mine eye." Then if we desire his company, we shall reply, " As the eyes of servants look unto the hand of their masters, and as the eyes of a maiden unto the hand of her mistress ; so our eyes wait upon the Lord our God." (Ps. cxxiii. 2.)

I knew a Christian lady whose health was greatly reduced by indefatigable nursing, but who denied herself the most necessary comforts, and whose evident need touched my heart keenly. We had a mutual friend, — one who truly walked with God, — possessed of ample means, and with them a most generous heart. On one occasion our poor sister confessed her need, yet to my surprise and sorrow my friend did nothing toward relieving it, nor did she express any peculiar sympathy on the occasion. Perhaps from some feeling of disappointment that one ordinarily so quick to feel for others should in this case withhold her ready resources,

I judged her hastily, and I gave at once what I had, without any consideration or prayer. I had not then learned — and we often need our lessons repeated — that all we possess is the Lord's, and we have no right to dispose of it according to our fancy or feeling, and that we miss great blessing when we lack his guidance in its distribution, whether it be of the value of one pound or fifty, or fifty pence or five. I did not often see our poor friend after this ; but though I knew there were other sources of help open to her, I always observed the same necessities. She seemed to have lost all joyfulness in the manifest tokens of the Lord's care for her. She died. After her decease we found she had a relative who was very dear to her : he had been a gambler. The money given for her own use, to prepare her by rest and change to continue her vocation, had been given to pay his gambling debts. The friend I had judged unjustly had no more information in regard to her private circumstances than I had ; but she *walked with God*, and in seeking his guidance as to what sum she might give, she saw that she must withhold her succor altogether, for it was not according to the mind of the Lord.

The Lord knoweth the heart, and none else. He can supply every need ; and if we keep ourselves at his disposal, He will not fail to use us. If He allows us the inestimable privilege of carrying his messages and his blessings, his gold and his silver, his counsel and his comfort to the needy, let us praise Him for such goodly service, and be able to say, " Of Thine own have we given Thee " ; but do not let us suppose that we give of store in our own possession, for He will show us that it is not in man that walketh to direct his steps.

There is faith needed in receiving as well as in giving, whether it be the things of time, or the things eternal and invisible. The grace we plead for, we receive by faith, and the same faith is needed for every good gift: but like Elisha with Elijah's mantle, we must test the power we have prayed for by making use of that within our grasp ; and if we have prayed for faith, be sure we shall have opportunities of proving it. Among my failures — and their name is legion — I remember being deeply moved by hearing of a tradesman who had been unjustly accused and thrown into prison on evidence eventually discovered to be false. He was a Christian living among those who were not favorable to him on that account. When he left the prison, which he did with unblemished character, no one would trust him with the needful materials for recommencing his trade. " In prison ! " — and he was shunned by all. He was industrious and a good workman, and would soon have repaid a loan ; but work he had none : credit was gone, and neighbors scoffed. No matter to them if he deserved or did not deserve the jail, he had been there, and he and his wife must bear the reproach and perish. I heard of him ; he lived far away from the place where I then resided. I was used of the Lord to help him with a small sum of money, most clearly impressed on my heart to send him ; the time, the amount, both marked by One who knew best what he required of me. The gratitude of the sorely tried pair for this timely help came to my heart in an hour of peculiar trial, and made sunshine in a shady place.

Later, some money was paid me unexpectedly. *I took the circumstance for my guide*, without seeking for the Counsel ever at hand to direct, or praying that I might be guided in the matter as I had been previously; and only thinking of their extremity and the pleasure of giving. I sent the man five pounds. thinking that this would enable him to commence his trade, independent of his neighbors. I had made myself a Providence; and though in many cases the Lord overrules our blunders and our sins for eventual good, in this case I had to learn one of my first lessons in giving. The eye of the Lord is on every living thing: He giveth according to their real need; for He has ever before Him the eternal gain, which we see not.

I heard no more of the poor tradesman for a long time. Then a letter reached me from a friend, who had first told me of his trouble, inquiring if I had been unfortunate enough to lend this poor man a Bank-of-England note for five pounds. Before his conversion, he had been a drunkard; but for years he had been restored. He was led to change the note at a tavern. The sight of the money, most likely, induced the landlady to invite him to drink. He consented, never intending it to be more than the offered glass. Perhaps the apparent cordiality of those who had shunned him was too much for him. Who knows? But he drank on until the money was expended, and he was worse off than before; the poor wife desolate, the husband fallen, and the testimony he had once given the scorn of the drunkards! And for all this I was unwittingly the cause, because I had not relied on my heavenly Counsellor to guide me to do his will. True, the temptation might have been presented by another; *that* is not given to us to know. Enough, that *my* hands had put the means in his power to fall into the snare, — a snare wrought out in *natural* benevolence ; and in place of saving him from evil, I had hastened on the day of his humiliation. And though he was restored and taught his own weakness by this act of weakness, through my inconsiderate generosity, yet I had unwittingly caused him to err. I believe that natural benevolence unchecked causes as much sorrow as the miserly spirit that sees a need and does not help it.

I suffered acutely from this circumstance ; for I did *not* walk with God. If I pray for gold, and I receive gold, it is tangible ; I can display it to my neighbors, and exchange it for whatever I need. But there are requests granted which it would be in vain to spread before others, because they could not know their value to us. So there are graces and blessings we yearn for and pray for, that we do not share with our dearest friends. But all these secret needs draw us nearer to Him who loves us, not as a Benefactor, but as a Father who desires to see us growing into the likeness of the only perfect One.

I know a devoted clergyman of the Church of England who lacked faith to cast himself on the teaching of the Holy Spirit for delivering the message of the Lord ; yet he was continually praying for deliverance from the bondage of his written discourses. His sermons were carefully prepared, but always lacked the freedom which he longed for. He had been passing through a season of conflict and darkness, — known to those "who do business in great waters," — from a highly nervous temperament. His suffering had been acute and his despondency great. His distress deepened as the hour drew on at which he was engaged to preach in a distant town. He arrived at the place only in time to ascend the pulpit. He had hardly done so, when he discovered that his sermon was missing! He had lost it on the road! It was impossible to supply its place. With a cry of distress to the Lord *Almighty* to help him in his extremity to speak to the large congregation before him, his eye fell on Isaiah viii. 17 : " *I will wait upon the Lord, that hideth his face from the house of Jacob, and I will look for Him.*"

From the dire conflict and experiences through which he had been led, floods of light opened to his admiring soul, giving him a knowledge of God's way and God's love. A live coal from the altar had touched his lips, and from the fire kindled in his own breast, his hearers were moved as never before. He never read his sermon again! But for this time of tribulation and the necessity of throwing himself on the Lord, he would have lost the power that waited only to be used. Thus he was blindly led to obtain the thing he desired, while the season of proving prepared him for the result. How much blessing we miss when we act without taking counsel of the Lord; and what knowledge of Him and his ways is imparted to us when patiently, diligently, prayerfully we wait upon Him for counsel, and walk with Him! It is very easy to employ our natural gifts without this, and act with apparent gener-

osity, sympathy, and munificence, and find in the end
that, like Joshua (ix. 14), we have entertained, not
an angel unawares, but an enemy in the camp; and
though such are good hewers of wood and drawers of
water when employed by the Lord for his work, they
are often sources of repentance when used solely for
our own satisfaction. We should have escaped the
snare that entrapped us if we had " asked counsel" of
Him " who giveth liberally and upbraideth not," and
not walked according to our " own understanding."
(Prov. viii. 5.)

Providences of God, and our well-meant but self-
ordained providences, are very different in effect, both
on our own soul and on that of the recipient, as well as
in the ultimate issue. Though fair to outward view,
they are often numbered among the transgressions to
be blotted out by the blood of the Lamb. When the
Lord has made use of my weakness, and even my little
faith, I can look back with a song of rejoicing; though
when I have testified to the power manifested through
the simplest means, men without faith have mocked!
But the scorner cannot rob me of my blessing by his
scorn, nor the Lord of his honor; and I can pity those
who ostensibly accept the Lord Jesus Christ as the
Saviour, — " specially of those who believe, " — and yet
find no delight in watching for his guidance, observing
his hand, listening for his voice, and tracing his footsteps.

The importance of the work of the Spirit is far too
little cherished and considered in daily life. The great
tendency of the age is for sight, not faith, or grasping

the privileges of the gospel without any experience of its power; and much teaching that seems fair is entirely adapted to promote these states. Faith in the revealed power of God is virtually made a lie. God says, "Believe and be saved," and he that believes accepts the great salvation; and men who believe not, say it is impossible to know whether he is saved or lost until he is gathered to heaven or cast into hell! whether his good works have sufficiently atoned for his sins, or whether what the Lord Jesus declared is true, "Whosoever believeth on Me, though he were dead, yet shall he live"! So in walking with God, those who have not sought an understanding heart do not believe in his promises of walking with his people, and guiding them in their way: believe not, because they seek by nature what is given to faith only. They will declare, "It is the Lord," when the results are according to their own desires; but when the consequences of their action are other than they expect, they doubt the care of Him who was never trusted in vain. *I* have never "trusted in Him and been confounded." Have you?

The interior light, which is often given in prayer and ¡n many cases spontaneously, for guidance, does not set at naught all outward evidence of this way. Such are often encouragements to proceed in paths we should not have chosen for ourselves, and to confirm and strengthen our faith in that which the Holy Spirit has opened to us. Those who seek shall *find*. The Lord has thousands of means to make his *will* evident, but the *way* may open slowly. I have often been troubled when I have desired to do the Lord's will, to find the results quite other than I hoped for; this is judging by *sense*. He knows what He needs done, both in our souls and for others; but we must be upright before Him, and then, though we may have trouble in the flesh, we shall be at peace with Him.

I received a letter from a stranger that would have moved my heart to tears from its contents. I grieved that I was prevented from replying, and full of compunction that I could let several days elapse without expressing my sympathy. When I spread the letter before the Lord, all my sympathy seemed shut up in my breast, and I wrote what appeared to me a severe rebuke. When the letter was gone I was very sorrowful, and never expected to hear again. Yet long after this I received a letter from the writer, thanking me for my faithful rebuke, though in truth I remembered nothing but that I had written what seemed a very needlessly harsh letter; but the Lord saw beneath the surface, and used my unwilling hand to wound and not to sympathize, to rebuke and not comfort. That letter was of inestimable price to me in showing me the power of God, if we would only trust Him to " work in us " and for us.

I remember hearing one exclaim, " There is no difficulty in walking with God." I asked, " Do you walk with God?" " Yes," she replied. " And how do you walk with Him?" " Why, of course I think of Him when I walk out." And I believe many suppose that in taking a journey or beginning some evident enterprise, in seeking help, they " walk with God." But to walk with God we need the continual realization of his love. The great want of the church is personal intimacy with the Son of God, and this springs from faith and love in the Father who gave Him, and the Holy Ghost who manifests Him. "No man cometh unto the Father but by Me." (John xiv. 6.) "All things are delivered unto Me of my Father, neither knoweth any man the Father save the Son, and he to whomsoever the Son will reveal Him" (Matt. xi. 27); and "in Him dwelleth all the fulness of the Godhead bodily" (Col. ii. 9). The man of understanding "walketh uprightly," but we know it is the "*hearing heart*" by which alone he can do it. "Blessed is the man that heareth Me"; he it is that receiveth knowledge which only fools hate.

Solomon did not think the least possession of an "understanding heart" was "to do justice and show mercy" to the oppressed, and this can only be done in "truth and equity" with light from within. In 2 Chron. xx. 23, it is told us of the wisdom God had put into his heart; and we know that Christ *abiding* in us, we have the wisdom of God and the power of God to supply our ignorance and our weakness. "He that believeth on Me," as the Scripture hath said, "out of his belly shall flow rivers of living water." "I am come a light into the world, that whosoever believeth on Me should not *abide* in darkness," but should have the light of life. (John xii. 46.)

To know God, — this is the purpose of the understanding heart. If the "wisdom of God" were only required for ruling, or understanding what we see, then the gift of Solomon would be set forth to kings and rulers only;

.

but it is needed for all, — for all conditions, all times, all things ; for the knowledge of God is attained through the wisdom and power of God. " *The knowledge of the holy is understanding.*" (Prov.) It is through the knowledge of Him who is the fountain of all wisdom that men live, not by works ; it is through faith *in* Him in whom we abide that the invisible is manifested by works to " them that are without," so that those that have eyes may see, and those that have ears may hear.

While Solomon sought the glory of the Lord with an upright heart, he prospered ; but when idols and those who worshipped idols found a place in his heart, he worshipped *them*, and forsook the Lord his God, who had appeared unto him twice. It is possible to make an idol of our gifts, of our faith or knowledge, as well as an idol of one in whom God's gifts are manifested. If you rest on your gifts and the success that may have attended them, you will fall ; but if you keep them at the feet of the Master, ready for any case He may ordain, you will abide with *Him* for *his* work (1 Chron. iv. 24), and not for *your* gifts or work. Solomon had wisdom and knowledge unsurpassed of all the men that were before or came after him ; and the wisdom God put into his heart was the *answer to prayer.* That wisdom enabled him to rule a great people ; it brought him riches and honor : but it did not keep him from the influence of " strange women," who ensnared him in idolatry. " *Let him that glorieth, glory in this, that he understandeth and knoweth Me.*" (Jer. ix. 24.) If we make idols, though we value them for their gifts and grace, we shall fall, and we may thus become a snare to them and cause them to fall. God is a jealous God, and will not give his glory to another. Forgetting the Giver in the gift, we are certain to bring sorrow to them, as well as to ourselves. God will show that not in man, but in Jesus only, are " laid up " the treasures of might and wisdom.

The apostles everywhere warned those who beheld the miracles, and would exalt the workers (Acts iii. 12), " Why marvel ye at this? or why look ye so earnestly on us as though by our own power or holiness we had made this man to walk? " The weakest and least " comely members " are generally chosen for the most evident manifestation of the Spirit; and none of us have aught to glory in. The only true knowledge is to know Him, and the only wisdom is to abide in and with Him. To follow Jesus we need no other model. There is only one original that can be safely copied ; and when He is our example, there is originality in the copy, though millions copy it.

We may imitate the life principles of those honored and blessed of God, but not the life itself, which must differ in every individual. The faithful followers of Christ have the same end in view, but how varied the circumstances in which they " walk with God "! How diversified the gifts, the trials and temptations on the way! Some have learned their task in tears ; while some, with hardy faith not given to all, have dashed the tears away and learned to love the cross that gave some new view of Him they desired to know more perfectly. Some have been taught the utter abomination of their natural heart, by inbred corruption thrown out-

ward to sight, like the loathsome leper ; and some, like
Jairus's daughter, have *appeared* only awakened into
life by light and love : yet the same lesson, first or
last. must be learnt by all, — to *know Him ;* and by the
grace He *waits* to give, will manifest Himself through
you.

Beyond the grace for salvation and the fruits of
the Spirit, are special gifts of grace, as seen in the
faithfulness of Abraham, the meekness of Moses, the
patience of Job. There are also gifts accorded to
special needs and circumstances and positions to
which the Lord calls his people. We trace this in the
statesmanship of Joseph, for which he had received no
training in his father's house nor in his prison ; in
Nehemiah's architectural science ; and aforetime in
Bezaleel's marvellous knowledge for the work of the
tabernacle, engraving, embroidery, and weaving, cutting of precious stones and carving of wood, to shadow
forth the mystery of the glorious redemption, and the
law's requirements, yet to be fulfilled by the spotless
Lamb.

With these gifts are the open doors to exercise
them in the sight of man for testimony. God gave
Joseph favor in the sight of the keeper of the prison,
and afterward grace in the sight of the king, to place
him where the gift should be used for the protection
and deliverance of Israel. Daniel had skill and spiritual understanding of secret things, whereby he was
to testify of the living God, whom he served in the
court of kings. For this he must be brought a captive
to a heathen nation, to whom he must witness (and

to witness is to suffer), as well as to be the appointed recipient of the mysteries of the future Kingdom. God brought Daniel into favor and "tender love" with the prince of the eunuchs. The servant of the living God must be tried and proved : and the rage and envy and hatred of the princes, and the lion's den, was the ordained position of the "man greatly beloved," to enable him to glorify the God whom he "served continually."

The unlettered men who went forth as witnesses of their risen Lord displayed more than any others the power of God by the eloquence of their discourses, and the bold delivery of their message, with the gift of tongues. They walked with God. Why, then, do we sit down discouraged and dismayed when we have such a *reality* to deal with? A reality — not an influence or a doctrine, but a person ! — who can endow us with the skill and understanding needful for every service to which we are called, can open the prison doors, defend us in the den of lions, and save us in the tabernacle of his presence from the scourge of the tongue, and give us favor in the sight of our enemies, for the accomplishment of his purposes. Above all things, let us remember that we are ever the care of Him whose "eyes run to and fro throughout the whole earth, to show *Himself* strong in the behalf of them whose heart is perfect toward *Him*." He saith, "My ways are not as your ways, nor my thoughts as your thoughts." But if your desire is for his glory, He will fulfil your desire, for it is born of the Holy Spirit. "Only be strong and very courageous." If you walk with Him, He will be with you in the fiery furnace and the den of lions. Your enemies are his enemies ; and though the way He leads may be to a prison or to death, yet the very hairs of your head are all counted, and not one can fall without his permission. The Lord keeps special consolations for special seasons of sorrow, and the heavenly manifestation of Himself for the hour of greatest difficulty, loneliness, and distress. It is the most humiliating of all experiences that these gracious testimonies of his love and care cannot forever crush the evil heart of unbelief, and that the tender compassion of our faithful Friend so often finds us faithless and afraid. He does not pour the wine for those whose hearts are glad, and only the wounded know the tenderness of the pierced hand, that pours in the oil and binds up the wound. He keeps his personal consolations for those bitter sorrows that have no comforter, and his immediate counsel for those who have no earthly counsellor in their need.

I have often observed that when we have a friend in sympathy with us, if we require help, God ordinarily makes use of that instrument and withholds immediate heavenly comfort. It is possible even at these times to find the word of God as it were sealed to us, and prayer a difficulty and a task, not a joy as heretofore. It is the emptying of the vessel by making it feel the utter poverty of all we possess out of Christ Himself. He has shown me that if we " set our affection on things above, where Christ sitteth on the right hand of God," we may be sorrowful and tempted and barren, but nevertheless we can still rejoice in the *Lord*, for He is the object of the longing soul, of all our desires, of all our hopes.

Where our treasure is there will our heart be also; and where God's treasure is, there will *his* heart be also. Do not let Satan rob you of this assurance. Though the Heavenly Shepherd seems a long way off, He keeps a watch over his flock by night; and though you cannot see Him, He can see *you*, and knows that your heart is desolate and afraid. Yes, we *have* this treasure in earthly vessels, and God has *his* treasure in earthly vessels, and He *knows* too the dust that composes them; but He has set his love upon them, and " none shall pluck them out of his hand."

I was called upon to take a voyage to Sicily. The storms at that season of the equinox were very frequent on the Mediterranean; and by some insufficient direction of the time of departure, I took the longest route, which forced me to make the whole journey by sea, which I would gladly have avoided. To take my passage I arrived at a cold, dreary hotel on the coast of Italy. I was quite alone, with a room where it was not possible to have either stove or fire. The cold wind and drenching rain and outward desolation made it truly a time of such a necessity for a realized sense of the Lord's mind, that I strove to watch day by day to know his will clearly. There was no outward duty, no external sign that I should undertake this particular voyage; nothing but the interior light: but the dealing of the Lord to bring about the act of obedience in regard to time was very strong and very close.

A poem I had just sent to press — "The Shining

Footsteps"—came to my mind while my heart was occupied in seeking guidance on my next step towards a winter shelter. Palermo rose constantly before me. As it was pronounced indispensable that I should pass the winter in a southern climate, there was nothing remarkable to others in that Sicily should have been presented to me. I went forward after much conflict, thankful that the way was so far clear, though a long and fatiguing voyage lay before me.

The morning after my arrival at the port, I awoke with the thought of Peter walking on the waters; and the words came to my lips, " *But when he saw the wind boisterous, he was afraid.*" Yet not once did this cross my mind as a preparation for myself; so naturally are we inclined to imagine that if the Lord calls us to follow Him. we must expect clear skies and waveless waters! So I looked for the clouds to roll away and to be followed by a voyage to the place appointed me. But every step must have its preparation for the next. Influenza laid me low, and I could not venture out of the house to obtain information of any other vessel sailing later. I quote from my journal : —

Tuesday. — " Rain pours in torrents and the wild waves dash up to the summit of the lighthouse, roaring on again and sweeping into the ocean ; everything around dark and dreary. Can it be possible that I have made a mistake? "—As I wrote these words, like a roll of sweet music rang through my soul, " *Cast not away therefore your confidence, which hath great recompense of reward.*" Then came a precious word, opening out the passage which follows, which is too frequently severed from the context and quoted alone : " *For* ye have need of *patience*, that, *after* ye have done the will of God. ye might receive the promise." (Heb. x. 35, 36.) "The Lord knows that my natural desires are not towards Palermo. He knows, too. that his grace and power alone draw me to follow Him. If He holds the sea in the hollow of his hand, He holds me (a great coward) ; therefore it must be well with me, come what will. The vessel sails to-morrow and I must go !"

Wednesday. — The storm ceased, and the wintry sunshine spread over the green sea for an hour. I went forth and purchased my ticket. The steward assures me that if the vessel should not sail, it would be available for another day. This cold, comfortless hotel and increasing influenza are an incentive not to tarry, but to press forward to the sunny shores of Sicily.

Thursday. — Did not leave my bed until dinner, and went down to the *table d'hôte* sad at heart. My neighbor was a bright-faced Scotch lady of noble presence ; and as she was inclined to converse, I spoke of my dear Master, of his goodness and his power and his faithfulness : and I was at once refreshed and strengthened, as the heart always must be in drawing nearer to the Source of Strength. There were only seven or eight people besides ourselves at the table. Suddenly I found every one was listening ; and strange to say, without cavil or contempt. My neighbor was a Christian, and our conversation became more intimate. She introduced me to her husband, the Laird of B——, who was very cordial ; and as he rose from the table, he gave me their card, and hoped we should meet again. With my heart raised by this brief fellowship, I retired to my room to make my last preparations for the voyage. In a few minutes, the kind friend so unexpectedly provided for me followed me to invite me to their *salon*, as the boat did not sail until midnight. Gladly I accepted the invitation, and followed her into one of the lofty rooms of the old *palazza*. A bright wood fire, with its cheerful blaze, lighted up the frescos and mirrors, and the antique furniture glowed. I spent more than an hour seated between two of my Father's family, telling them of Him whose exceeding grace had won me from death unto life and light. They listened with unabated interest. Before I left, they told me that they felt our meeting was of the Lord, and that I had been sent to tell them that everywhere is service for the child of God, which it had been difficult to realize in foreign travel. Many little packages of useful articles were arranged for my journey, for my comfort, which they thought I really needed.

Like myself, supposing that if the Lord had called me to follow *Him*, the boisterous sea would be still again, and the winds, now lulled to rest, would rise no more, they both escorted me to the door of the hotel, and the lady embraced me tenderly at parting; while the laird, though an invalid, insisted upon accompanying me to the quay. To strengthen my confidence, my kind escort told me he had lived a yachting life, and knew the Mediterranean *well;* and I must not judge of the open sea by the rough waves near land, as after a few miles we should be in still waters. So we parted, *he* to his pleasant companion and cheerful fire, and I to the boat which was to convey me to the vessel, with a starless sky above and the dark waters beneath.

It pleased me to believe, in despite of my senses, that the heavy clouds that rose and gathered on the deep-blue darkness of the Italian sky would soon pass away when we had left the haven. I had yet to learn, like Peter, that it is easier to follow the Lord on dry land than on the water. I shrank from the sea, that, though quieter, was still ominous with its quick swell. Text after text arose to cheer me as I stood waiting by my luggage on the boat, and as I laid hold of each promise, they became like links in a chain to draw me onward and upward; and so I entered the boat that was to convey me on board. We came to a bridge which was under repair, and threatened danger from the scaffolding compelled the sailors to steer very carefully by the light of their lantern. They bade me lie down in the boat to the very lowest, for only so could we pass safely under the arch. I did so.

Suddenly there came to my mind a vision of the night when I beheld a little boat in just such darkness, beneath the low arch of a bridge lighted by a single lantern. I saw a chest, such as is used for plate; it was hidden and carried on board so carefully and tenderly, it was evidently some precious freight; with faded chintz covering, worn and ragged. As the breeze lifted the drapery which concealed it, I beheld, on the centre of the lid, a tiny flame of a lamp, unprotected, burning and flickering as the night passed over it; yet the fragile covering was not consumed, nor the light extinguished. As it approached me, it appeared like the ark of the covenant; and as I marvelled why, I beheld ah and of exceeding beauty that moved every way to shield it from the blast. As the rough men carried it on board, people on land inquired, " Why all this care for this burden?" and a voice from a cloud, in the direction of the hand, replied, " It is the King's treasure." Yes: where God's treasure is, there will his heart be also; and the worn casket, of little worth for all else, was still dear to God. So He comforted me, speaking not " once " nor " twice," but many times.

I could not take my berth previously, as it was possible the weather might prevent the vessel from leaving the port; as there were likely to be few passengers, it seemed of no account. The cold wind swept over me as I ascended the vessel's side; the darkness increased from the gathering clouds. The desolation of my soul who can tell! Like Peter, my eyes were on the billows and the coming storm, and not on my Master, who had bade me *come unto him on the water;* therefore it was no marvel that I began to sink.

The state-room held several Italian women already in bed, who assailed me with abuse for disturbing them to take possession of the vacant berth. I applied for another small private cabin which I had seen was vacant, that I might be alone; it was rudely refused me, so I laid down in the berth indicated for me. The insolence of the woman who acted as stewardess, the night wind blowing on my chest from the open door, and a lamp with its sharp rays close and directly in my eyes nearly distracted me, and my persecutors would not allow the door to be closed nor the lamp to be moved. Then the storm broke; and such a storm! Within and without, sickness began, and spasms. I sprang from my berth in agony, and as I fell from one stay to another to the ground, I was greeted with shouts of laughter and mocking from the women around.

The Lord had written, " Call upon Me in the time of trouble; I will deliver thee." But oh for the faith and patience by which we inherit the promises! I cried to the Lord to still the storm, — it rose wilder; to relieve me of my sufferings, — they increased. Rebellion awoke a storm within more terrible than the one without. The enemy whispered, "God does not hear prayer; you are all to die!" Despair rolled over my soul! I remember little more than that I found myself in the cabin which had been refused me, and a kind-looking man, with earnest solicitude, leaning over me, feeling of my pulse. The storm still raged in fury *without*, but the Saviour walked on the rough billows of my soul; it was "the fourth watch of the night." The vessel shook, crashed, rolled, but the vigorous grasp of my kind nurse prevented me from being dashed to the ground. There seemed nothing but death before us. — Jesus was there! There was a great calm.

The captain came for a moment and looked on me, and ordered hot-water bottles to be placed to my feet, and slices of hot lemon bound around my head. As he bent down to my pillow I inquired, " Is there danger? " He answered in French, — I thought evasively, — " The vessel is a good one; it was builded in England." As he passed from my cabin I heard the terrified women in the state-room shrieking and crying, some thrown from their berths, and one seriously injured; and I safe in my little cabin! — not for *my faith and patience*, but for Jesus' sake, by the exceeding grace of God, accepted in the Beloved, who gives to the unthankful and rebellious out of the riches He died to secure to his own. I know not what office my kind nurse held in the vessel, but they addressed him " Padrone "; but *this* long night, watch was kept over me. When the spasm convulsed my frame, he held me gently but firmly, saying " Coraggio! coraggio! " and so the night wore on.

I did not fear death; it had no shadows for me. Jesus was walking upon the waters. He had answered my prayer: He had sent me help in my distress, and not delivered me out of it! He had his own purposes in it all; and who was I that I could withstand God? I prayed for the friend He had sent me in " the time of trouble." I could only ask Him to have his services in everlasting remembrance! The storm abated. I opened my eyes and saw my kind nurse, who had quitted me for other duties, again by my side. He said gently, " You have been sleeping? " " Not so," I answered, " I was praying for you." He did not say as some do, " Thank *you*, you are very kind." Silently he raised his cap and remained some moments uncovered; and then the eyes of the Italian were uplifted with an expression of gratitude as he said, " Grazia, grazia, O Dio Salvatore! "

Then the Lord's own voice was heard louder than the voice of many waters, — " It is I, be not afraid." My heart bounded with joy as I eagerly inquired, " Do you, then, love Jesus and pray to *Him?*" "Oh, yes!" he replied quietly, as a smile of inexpressible sweetness passed over his face; "morning and evening and midday, up on deck and down here, among all sorts of people, and alone. . . . What would my life be without *Him?*"— (I thought I had caught the word "Madonna.")

Thirty-nine hours of tempest now left only a heavy ground swell. I was alone, but from time to time my kind nurse came and assured himself of my safety, bringing me some strong soup, with which he fed me by spoonfuls as if I were a sick child.

We could not reach the harbor, so the passengers were compelled to land far from the quay in the open sea. The boats received the passengers, and again I was on the sea; but though it was boisterous, I was not afraid. The Lord's hand had been so far manifested. As my friend bade me farewell, he inquired if he could be of service to me, and sent an attendant with me, and advised me to go to another hotel than that which I had clearly seen set before me. Therein I walked according to the counsel of man, and not according to the light already given me, and won for myself darkness and distrust.

I passed a few nights of peculiar trial and testimony in Palermo, partly from walking according to nature and not by faith. But the Lord, faithful and true, did not forsake me; but by forsaking his counsel I missed the link in the chain, and the blessing which enables us to see more of the glory of the Lord, in the fellowship which neither trials nor sorrow nor rejection nor persecution can hide from us. All things work *together* for good to them that love Him; but the "working together" often ploughs up the depths of the heart and proves the innermost motives of action. It was once said by an aged Christian as her wilderness experience, that "one step out of the way will take forty steps to bring you back to the turning point." Still, by the grace of Him who ever liveth to make intercession, the Lord did meet me with blessing.

Previously to leaving Palermo, I became acquainted with a missionary who visited the vessels in port. I prayed him to seek my kind night-watcher, and tell him that I was going to Catania; and if the vessel went there, to remember his promise to visit me. Accordingly, many weeks after I had been at Catania, I received a message that my kind friend would come the next time the vessel sailed.

Two years before, a lady had given me an Italian Bible. For what purpose she had been led to purchase it she could not tell, as she had no knowledge of the language nor any expectation of going to Italy (neither had I at that time) ; but when she offered it me, I accepted it, believing that a way would be found for disposing of it : and now its destination seemed very plain. Fever, which had laid me down the previous spring, broke forth at intervals ; but my sojourn was a pleasant one, so by living much in the air I thought to overcome it : but in vain. My eyes were unto the Lord to know what I should do and where I should go, and I watched for the indication of his will ; but the door was still closed and not a bolt withdrawn.

The glory of a Sicilian spring had broken with cloud-less skies, with its gorgeous flora, and its balmy breeze from the sea; but my strength failed day by day. I watched and waited, and was able to believe that He who had led me *this* time so that I did not stumble, would open the door when the "set time" was come. I was no longer capable of exertion, nor did I see what to do. One evening, after a day of intense heat, a visitor was announced, and my Italian friend stood before me with the frank and kindly greeting that enabled me at once to enter on that which was so nigh to my heart.

Our parting had been amid the roar of the billows, with the drifting clouds of the early morning carried over the gray sky, with the weary faces and loved voices, and the cries of the boatmen around the vessel; and now we met in the stillness of a Sabbath evening, with the cloudless blue sky above us, with the faint lines of a spring sunset stealing over it, and lightening the white peaks of Etna with its rosy hues. The wide expanse of lava lay around, partly clothed with the olive and the prickly pear, and all blended beneath the golden glow that marks the climate of Southern Sicily. It seemed like the contrast of the "land of the dying" with the "land of the living," — "the night of weeping" with the "morning without clouds," — when the weary desert pilgrims, sheltered at last in the haven of Home, shall commune together with the Lord who led them, of the mercies of the way, and join in the song of Moses and the Lamb. Perhaps something of the same thought passed through the mind of the Italian, for an expression of full content spread over his face as he silently surveyed my little *salon*, and then from the balcony looked out on the distant sea and the snowy mountain, and again his eyes rested on me ; and then, as if he had pondered on the strange providence that had brought me there, he said slowly and emphatically, " You will not die here ! "

" No," I answered, " I have yet work to do."

" Work," he repeated in amazement, " what work can you do?"

" The Lord needs the weak ones, and thus I can work for Him ; little have I done for Him, though I have known Him for fourteen years."

" But He knew you long before that," he observed, with a bright smile.

We might have been old acquaintances, so quickly grows the bond of fellowship in the eternal reality of a *living* Saviour. Had it been a case for argument I was unfitted for it, but none was needed ; it was simply a reception of that for which his heart was prepared and which he gladly accepted. Educated on the sea, alone with the Great Teacher, it was one of the mysteries we cannot solve to hear the record of the simple faith that overleaped the superstition of his country and rested in " *Jesus only.*" I possess nothing wherein I can boast, but certainly a more unsuitable instrument could hardly have been chosen, according to sight, — my hoarse, broken voice in the midnight storm, and now with scarcely energy to rise from my couch ; yet the feeblest can set before a soul the fulness in the power of the blood of the Lamb slain, and the faithfulness of Him whose fidelity we have proved.

When I paused, fearing that he did not comprehend all I longed for him to see as part of his heritage, he smiled at my fears. Pressing his hands on his breast, he repeated more than once, " I understand *all* you wish me to know — ALL : I feel it *here.*" The Lord had given power to the faint, and to them that have no might He increased strength. As I placed the Bible in his hands I felt the Lord was there ; and believing, Jesus had entered into the boat ; and we knew Him whose paths are on the deep waters and whose footsteps are not seen.

It might be argued, by those who know not the leading of the Lord, that a colporteur might have been used to carry the Bible to one who received it gladly. But a colporteur could not have done my work, neither could I have done his.

Before leaving, he urged me to quit the vicinity of the sea immediately for the Termini Mountains, and directed me in the means of recovery from the fever of the country, which the natives best know how to treat, and all with expression of the same kindly interest as when he had been *sent of God* to watch over me in a storm, when the deep waters had gone nearly over my head ; and now he was used to point me to the way I should go and the thing I should do, and I could follow and not be afraid, for I was listening only for the will of the Lord to be made known to me. And now the door was open and I could arise and go. He had promised, " Thine eyes shall see thy teachers : and thine ears shall hear a word behind thee, saying, This is the way, walk ye in it, when ye turn to the right hand, and when ye turn to the left." (Is xxx. 20, 21.) Like Peter, I had asked, " If it *be* Thou," and He had stretched forth his hand and saved me from sinking. " I am the Lord thy God, that divided the sea, whose waves roared : The Lord of hosts is his name." " O thou of little faith, wherefore didst thou doubt? " By faith and patience we inherit the promises. This is my heart's refrain on many a dark day. Those who *trust* in the *living God* are never confounded. But there are times when we are trusting to sense or means, and it is blessed when it is revealed to us, even through suffering, " Such as are upright in the way are his delight." But we are not always " upright," because we are not abiding ; and though the promises remain the same, we cannot then use them as such.

It would be more pleasant to the natural heart to receive distinct direction for our way, as given to Joshua (iv.), or when earthly resources fail, to receive the order that should guide us to the brook Cherith, even though the brook may dry up (1 Kings xvii. ; Judges vii. 9), or receive the command for our service (Luke xxii. 10, 11, 12 ; Acts ix. 11, 12, x. 19, 20). Yet, in a measure, if we walk by *faith* and not by sight, none ever lacked the voice of the Good Shepherd that goeth before his sheep. We may not see an " angel in the house, as did Cornelius," but the Lord of hosts has a thousand times ten thousand messengers. His angel providences and his human instrumentalities, and the visitor of Nehemiah in the palace of Shushan (Neh. i. 2), and the vision of the man of Macedonia, are alike from Him ; for He has many servants, and He saith unto one "Go," and he goeth, and to another "Come," and he cometh, and to his servant "Do this," and he doeth it : and to believe and despair not, to trust when not a rent of the clouds shall show light beyond, — this, this is faith ; this is giving honor to God.

Faith exercised by use proves experimentally the faithfulness of Him we trust, and this strengthens our confidence in his truth. So we learn to walk with God. When others see only a wall like a battlement in our way, so that we cannot pass over, we shall recognize an incentive to patient application and persevering prayer. When others pity us for an afflictive dispensation, we shall acknowledge it the wall of fire to hedge up our path to that goal which we could not have chosen for ourselves. We shall look back on past deliverances when He was our shield and buckler ; and we shall boldly say, "The Lord is my helper, I will not fear what man can do unto me." The Tempter will lay snares for you and strive to rob you of your confidence : but the blood is on the altar ; the sacrifice is slain ; the Son of God, son of David, the risen Lord, Emmanuel, ever liveth to make intercession for us.

CHAPTER VII.

" IVE me a blessing : for thou hast given me a south land ; give me also springs of water." (Judges i. 15.)

Is it your desire to honor the Lord? Then trust Him fully. He has promised, " Them that honor Me, I will honor." Are you crying, " As the hart panteth after the water brooks, so panteth my soul after Thee, O God. My soul thirsteth for God, for the living God "? Think you that He hears your cry unmoved? Behold Him stand, and hear Him cry, " If any man thirst, let him come unto Me and drink."

What was the heritage of Achsah? Even by faith! The daughter of one who wholly followed the Lord his God believes in the love and favor and power of that Father to bestow all she asks. The faithful Caleb, knowing the heart of his child, listens to her prayer, " Give me a blessing : for thou hast given me a south land ; give me also springs of water." Did he refuse it, and think she asked too much? He gave her the upper springs and the nether springs. (Joshua xv. 18, 19.)

Have you faith to ask and faith to *receive?* Then let *Him* choose your inheritance for you. You may drink of the brook by the way, and He may cause it to dry up; you may weep by the waters of Meribah and Marah; deep may call unto deep at the noise of His water-spouts; wells may be choked in the desert and rivulets lost sight of among the rocks: but if you are indeed thirsting for the living God, then believe that you do not thirst in vain. He that inciteth the thirst is about to supply from the great ocean of his love, into which flow the springs that run among the hills; all things shall bear witness of that living God whom you desire to "apprehend." (Phil. iii. 12.)

Is He the object of your life, the centre of your thoughts, the desire of your eyes? Do you turn to Him for repose and refreshment when weary and afraid? Then let Him share your household cares, your intimate joys, your hopes and fears. Then He will gird you for the battle, and show you the way in which He has called you to walk; He will walk with you in green pastures, and open your understanding that you may understand the Scriptures that testify of Him; He will be with you in your night vigil and your daily labor. For the soldier of the Cross, conflict is only over when the cross is borne no longer. He is to "resist the devil"; and who can resist him in his own strength? The rest of faith is to rest from our own works, and buckle on the armor of God, and fight the *good* fight, resting on Him who has conquered that we may obtain.

The daily duties that seem to deaden the soul by their formal recurrence form but a loom for the disciple of the glorious work of the Holy Spirit when kept beneath his influence. It is not needful to go out of the way to see his marvellous power, for only when we are *in* the way are its manifestations seen. There is no lot so dark and homely but is rendered glorious by the light of the dwelling ; none so full of care and daily burdens, but can be rendered a scene of triumph and rejoicing. In the obedience of faith you shall receive more than Caleb's daughter ; for the Father, on whose bounty you depend, giveth exceeding abundantly, above all you ask or think. If it tarry, wait for it. He has written in his tablet of love, " They shall not be ashamed that wait for *Me.*"

A young widow, a stranger, wrote to tell me the blessing she had received through some of my writings. The letter gave a touching history of her bereavement under peculiar and harrowing circumstances of sorrow ; but the bitter waters had become sweet by the hand of the Holy One, guiding the words I longed to write for many days, but from pain and sleeplessness I was unable. A night's sleep gave me life again, and it was clearly the Lord's will I should write. I did so. It was evening ; the light was fading as I sat to rest and asked a blessing on my written words. Clear and distinctly there came to me to order two books to be forwarded from England to my American sister. I looked at my watch : the hour for the courier leaving had passed ; my letter had already been sent. So surely that it was not of myself, I wrote the order on a post-card, and went to the mistress of the hotel to tell her my anxiety that it should leave that evening.

Though it was half an hour after the time appointed for the courier to leave, he had been detained! — the only day that he could remember this having happened — and he still stood on the door-step and received my card. As I heard his quick step on the gravel, and watched him through the shadows of the tall pepper-trees and olives, I reasoned within myself, " It is surely of God." He alone can so order it that these books shall reach his widowed child at the appointed time, and my letter carry the blessing I have asked. Perhaps I never more realized the work of faith that obeys without questioning, than at that moment. The heart of the widow had dwelt on the sorrowful past, and Satan came in to accuse ; her peace seemed a fantasy, her rejoicing in Christ self-righteousness. The joy of her heart had ceased ; her dance was turned into mourning. To whom could she go? Even to Him who came to heal the broken in heart, to preach deliverance to the captive, and recovering of sight to the blind.

As she lay down that night of the 24th of December, she prayed for his hand, once wounded for her sins, to rest on her troubled heart and bestow upon her the gift of peace. She earnestly pleaded for some special seal of his love to reach her on the coming Christmas morning. She slept, and seemed to wait alone in a deserted dwelling ; and as she looked out on the wide fields of snow that surrounded her, she beheld a messenger in the distance, who seemed to fly swiftly over the snow-drifts. On approaching the door the veil and mantle fell from the form, and displayed a face in which peace inexpressible beamed. She clasped the sad watcher to her warm, beating heart, and in that embrace a peace passing understanding filled her spirit, and she awoke in surprise at this heavenly calm that had taken the place of her despair. While she marvelled at this swift reply to her cry, the letter which was the arrow of deliverance of the very God of peace, and the gift the Lord had impelled me to send her, were placed in her hands, and remain unto this day a fruitful subject of thanksgiving.

It is not always that we gather immediately what we sow. The reaping day of many a weeping seed-time is yet to come : though it tarry, wait for it. The precious germ, overwatched with the patience of hope, shall bring forth sheaves for the reaper. We cannot always expect to see the fruition : the trying of our faith worketh patience ; let patience have her perfect work, — but be assured not one little grain is lost. The obedience of faith enriches the heart of the sower and gives glory to God. Most frequently that which is despised by man gives pleasure to Him whose way is perfect, and who has set before you to obey Him in those things which are contemptible to the natural man, because they are not spiritually discerned. " Under-standing is a well of life unto him that hath it," and " wisdom dwells with understanding." Not the wisdom of this world ; but your faith should not stand in " the wisdom of men, but in the power of God." Nothing more effectually defeats the insidious attacks of the Enemy than the immediate dealing with the Lord Him-self. The accuser whispers, " God heeds not : you have forsaken Him ; you have wandered too long ; your heart is cold ; your prayer is mockery ; you are unworthy." Yea, even so ! Nevertheless — the Lamb was slain on Calvary. Worthy the Lamb !

When trials and afflictions come, we need ask their message, for they spring not from the dust. It is possible to understand somewhat of their mission, though much will be hidden here. The smoke of the crucible and the smelting process does not reveal the person of the great Refiner : it is faith that knows He is there ; and we shall see his face and *afterwards* yield " the peaceable fruit of righteousness." Therefore " remember the former things of old : for I am God, and there is none else ; I am God, and there is none like me." As He was in the beginning, He is now, and ever will be. When we read the record of the lives of David, of Job, of Paul, and others, we can even here trace the Hand that fashioneth his instruments by many a stroke of the hammer, by many a touch of the chisel.

There is something indescribably touching in the record of the early life of the man after God's own heart. When driven from the court of Saul, David went to Samuel and told him all that Saul had done to him, and he and Samuel went and dwelt at Naioth. The Lord had given David a friend at court who loved him as his own soul ; and now when he fled from his infuriated father-in-law, he is constrained to the companionship of the prophet who had anointed him as the future king of Israel, who carried to him the Lord's messages, and doubtless had watched his dealings with one so signally chosen to stand before Him.

The Lord alone knew the necessity of rest and sympathy for one whom He had ordained to everlasting testimony.

When the future king dwelt at Naioth, doubtless it was for this purpose that he was driven from the court of Saul. We know not what unfolding of God's way, what instructions, what encouragement were there vouchsafed him from the prophet.

Can we not remember the murmurs that arose in our hearts when we were thrust out of some pleasant resting-place, and knew not until long after that it was the way of the Lord, who lovingly drove us from a place of danger that *we* too might find Samuel at Naioth, or something dearer than a Samuel, — even a closer communion with Him who anointed us and made us "kings and priests unto God," thus by every step preparing us for our future position in the Kingdom? He can give us the host of Jonathan when it is needed, and send a Samuel to shelter us. The Lord can deliver us from the lion, that goeth about seeking whom he may devour, with a subtlety more terrible than a jealous and tyrannical Saul.

"David went on his way and Saul returned to his place."

Better to go on your way a fugitive, with God for your guide, though you know not where He may lead you, than return to a place God has forsaken (Sam. xxvi. 25), the abode of your enemies and his.

If we would but consider that the hairs of our head are all numbered, that not one trouble can befall us that has not been foreseen by Him, that the purpose ordained in it must be fulfilled, that the power to protect and defend his own is not lessened, his love and care have not slackened, — all these dark threads shall work together in a wonderful harmony. These blessed records of a Father's love shall be read through countless ages by those brought out of much tribulation, with his name upon their foreheads and their names upon his heart. O troubled soul, take courage! If thou wilt believe, thou shalt see the glory of God. The passover is still eaten with bitter herbs, staff in hand, with loins girded, to follow the pillar of cloud through life's wilderness journey. Here we have no continuing city. We seek one not made by hands, an abiding one in the city of the Lamb.

MARAH.

"I will make a man more precious than fine gold." — Is. xiii. 12.

The bitter stream of Marah, —
How did I quail and shrink,
As thirsting in the desert,
I trembling stooped to drink!
I murmured, " Why this Marah
On my lone path to-day? "
No answer but the roaring
Of the wild wave on its way.

Thirsty, footsore, and weary,
Did He not hear my cry? —
The mighty God of Jacob,
Who triumphed gloriously;
Whose praises fill the echoes,
Whose mighty deeds are told,
In each day's march of mercy,
As wondrous as of old.

Three days, — y t all was silence,
    And glittering sand and drought;
Three days I watched and waited,
    And living waters sought.
Three days, — but all was desert,
    And sharp the burning blast,
Like a furnace breath swept o'er me; —
    Deliverance came at last.

Behold, and lo! beside me
    I marked a fair tree lie,
Marred by fierce hands that felled it
    So rude and ruthlessly.
I cast it in the waters,
    And the stream flowed softly on;
I drank that day of Marah, —
    Its bitterness was gone.

That tender plant, rejected,
    Hidden from sight, had lain,
Until from earth's dark chamber
    It rose to life again.
Three days, — and then it blossomed,
    And wondrous fruit it bore;
Its leaves are leaves of healing,
    And will be evermore.

And now I stand by Marah,
    Where once I shrank and feared:
Even those bitter waters
    His tenderness endeared,
And safe beneath His shadow
    My soul looks calmly on,
Till the day breaks on the mountain,
    And the desert march is done.

Beneath the Rock I rest me.
The stream is bright and sweet;
I drink from its deep waters,
And lave my dust-stained feet;
I fill my earthen pitcher
From the wavelets on the brink:
Is one athirst and weary?
Then let him come and drink.

I thank thee, Lord, for Marah:
Thy bitter mercies shine
With the radiance of Thy glory,
In this lone march of mine.
I thank Thee, too, for Elim,
The palm-tree and the well;
But I praise Thee more for Marah
Than my stammering tongue can tell.

Amongst some of the bitter mercies for which I shall praise the Lord through eternity is my homelessness, perhaps the greatest to one who knows the value of a quiet resting-place. But I have found in it fellowship with my Saviour, and his sympathy has sealed it as a mercy.

Before I had begun to follow Him without conferring with flesh and blood, I was called to undertake a long journey to the house of a relative I had not met for years, on a matter which, to the view of a friend I consulted, was pronounced a loss of time and strength and money. But I had sought the Lord's will in it, and the pressure on my spirit when I strove to abandon it was such that I had to disregard all human approbation and go.

I rested one night from my journey, when my host

informed me that I occupied the only spare room in the house, and that after the following day he should require it for his nephew, a young officer who had greatly distinguished himself in the Indian war and was then in London, — the Queen having appointed that day to give him audience, that he might receive at her hand the decoration for his gallantry, and immediately afterwards he would arrive at the house. I was amazed and afraid, like the disciples when they followed the Lord aforetimes; and fear is the offspring of unbelief. Questions arose in my heart: After all, had I been deluded into the belief that it was imperative that I came to this house, and the purpose for which I had taken the journey defeated? for I had not had time to think of it until I had rested. There was no house near at hand where I could lodge, only the village inn, of no inviting character. I was unfitted to travel farther. I sat helplessly before the Lord, with scarcely a prayer in my sinking heart, only a moan of desolation on my lips; yet it reached the ear of Him who had bade me go, and He had said, " I have surely seen the affliction of my people, and have known their sorrows.' Surely He knows them now, for He has borne them, and He knows mine. He knew that only the belief that He had bade me go had brought me just where I was; and though Satan strove to wrest from me that assurance, I was assured that the step I had taken was not for my own pleasure, but solely because it appeared the will of my Father which is in heaven.

That night I could not sleep; it is fresh in my memory as if yesterday. I looked out in the night on the old trees that surrounded the house, and up to the stars shining in their calm beauty, and from the stars to my scattered luggage, and felt I had not where to lay my head. Yet the Lord was working in the palace of kings to give me the rest I needed. Oh, to honor Him by trusting Him, not *because* there is a rent in the cloud, but because He has bade us *trust!* for "His eyes are upon the ways of man, and He seeth all his goings." (Job xxxiv. 21.) The letter bag brought a note from the young officer, appointing two days later for his arrival. I had two days, then, to think what I should do; but nothing came of it. Two days to trust the Lord more fully, but my faith sank and trembled; yet it was not quite extinct, and but the very circumstance that I was expected to leave made my way dark and desolate. Instead of the expected guest arrived a telegram. The Queen was ill at Windsor, could not receive the young officer, and he must now wait in London for further intimation of time and place. So I occupied the "spare room" until the Lord bade me rise and depart; for it was the Lord's, though man called it his. I had no blessing with any one under the roof, but in the neighborhood I was allowed to lead one to the feet of the Lord, who sent me to awaken a backslider from slumber, and to knit on a link that allowed me afterwards to set the light of life before a self-satisfied worldling; and this, but for my homelessness, I might never have done.

When all I was needed for was completed (though then I knew it not), my path was made to go elsewhere; and not until I had left the neighborhood for many weeks was the "spare room" required for the expected visitor. Perhaps if I had been strong and capable of travelling, or another place opened, I should have left hastily; but it would not have been the Lord's way, and so I should have lost blessing by being out of the way. Are we, then, to expect *results* for the obedience of faith? for certainly we are to believe in them. Whether we shall see them in this world or the world that is to come, we must leave to Him who bids us follow Him and fear not.

www.ingramcontent.com/pod-product-compliance
Lightning Source LLC
Chambersburg PA
CBHW030115030726
47498CB00007B/2389